YOU SHOULD NOT BE

A COLLECTION OF HORROR STORIES
STORIES
C.R. LANGILLE

Timber Ghost Press

You Should Not Be

A Collection of Horror Stories

by C.R. Langille

Copyright © 2024, C.R. Langille

Published by Timber Ghost Press

Printed in the United States of America

Edited by: Beverly Bernard

Front Cover Art & Design by: Greg Chapman

Back Cover and Interior Design: Timber Ghost Press

Print ISBN: 979-8-9883040-8-1

www.TimberGhostPress.com

"You Should Not Be" originally appeared in *Art & Sedition* (LUW Press, 2022)

"The Other Inside Me" originally appeared in *206 Word Stories: A Horror Anthology* (Bag of Bones, 2022)

"Rocky Mountain Hocus" originally appeared in *34 Orchard, Issue 4* (34 Orchard, 2021)

"Dead Man's Hand" originally appeared in *From the Yonder* (War Monkey, 2020)

"The Deep Timber" originally appeared in *They Walk Among Us* (42 Books, 2020)

"Home" originally appeared in *Strange Stories: Vol 1* (42 Books, 2019)

EARLY PRAISE FOR YOU SHOULD NOT BE

"C.R.'s short fiction packs a huge impact. In this collection, you can expect eerie stories that take on cosmic implications with a steadily building sense of dread. C.R.'s fresh take on weird fiction tropes leads to some genuinely terrifying moments." Betty Rocksteady, author of *Soft Places*

"It is no surprise that C.R. Langille's writing style is reminiscent of an outdoors guide. Taking us along wooded trails through fantasy, sci-fi, and horror, they deftly maneuver through genres, sometimes hitting us quickly in flash fiction and sometimes letting things linger long enough to question our own realities.

"As one might expect, the Utah-set stories are among my favorites and the most successful in this collection. Of particular note is 'Night of the Wormheads.' I will be picturing that story the next time I visit our shared home state." —T.J. Tranchell, author of *The Lamentations of Blackhawk*

"*You Should Not Be* is one of those collections you have to read more than once. Not just because Langille's stories are perfectly paced, not just because of the new mythologies expertly crafted, and not just because it's a masterclass in short fiction, but because it will leave you desperate for another taste of their work." — Caitlin Marceau, author of *This Is Where We Talk Things Out*

CONTENTS

Dedication — IX

1. "You Should Not Be" — 1

2. "The Great Joining" — 23

3. "Rocky Mountain Hocus" — 33

4. "Dead Man's Hand" — 48

5. "Follow Me" — 67

6. "The Angler" — 76

7. "Degrading" — 86

8. "Home" — 118

9. "The Other Inside Me" — 123

10. "Night of the Wormheads" — 125

11. "The Old Oak" — 148

12. "The Perpetual Dance" — 158

13. "The Deep Timber" — 163

Acknowledgments — 204

For the new fans of horror. May your journey into the darkness be memorable.

"You Should Not Be"

She had been someone once. Full of power. Full of focus. Many feared her wickedness and did their best to avoid her very presence. Then, there was darkness. A sinking darkness that consumed, only to regurgitate and consume again. She floated in that black lightless sea for what felt like eons, until her thoughts and memory faded to nothing and she was nothing.

Then there was pain.

It started in her throat, as if she had swallowed a thousand nails. Each breath came ragged and forced. Yet underneath the pain was elation. For she was alive when she should not be.

She sat upright, clutching her chest and coughing. Night had fallen, and only the single pale streak of moonlight punched through a hole in the castle wall to light the gloomy room.

That made her narrow her eyes, even through the excruciating struggle for air. Why was there a hole in her castle? She knew this place was hers, even though she couldn't recall her name. Yet, that fact, and the fact that the land was hers, was crystal clear in her mind. That wasn't the only thing she could recount... no, she could remember one other fact that settled in her marrow. She was a witch.

Not some potion-brewing hedge-witch. No, she was a *Witch*. One of the four. One to be feared.

So why was it that the darkness filled her with dread?

The Witch tried to stand, but as she did her joints popped and groaned. The very act of movement was agonizing. She finally made it to her feet, but the world spun in circles. She steadied herself by bracing against the wall, but as she did, the darkness closed in on her.

The Witch could no longer see to the corners of the room; however, there was something there. The hairs on the back of her neck tingled as she stared into the dark. Then, whatever it was moved. It scraped against the walls with a sickening slap of something wet against the stone.

Somehow or another, the Witch had escaped the darkness, and deep down on some basic level, she knew that wasn't allowed. She should not be.

The darkness had come to reclaim her.

She shuffled toward the beam of moonlight, fully aware that it was the only thing now that could offer any mote of protection. The shadows slithered and wriggled, closing in on her, and she couldn't help but wonder why she had awoken like this, ripped from the darkness only to end up in a place ruled by the same.

As the wet thing slapped against the floor, only feet away now, the Witch took a step back and nearly tripped over a bucket that had been haphazardly dropped upon the ground. Upon seeing it, memories flooded the Witch's mind. She had tried to steal some stupid little girl's shoes... No, they weren't hers. Those silver shoes had belonged to another Witch. The Witch of the East. But in the Witch's attempt to get the shoes, that brat had doused her with water from that bucket.

Instead of claiming her prize, she had melted alive and felt every excruciating moment of it until the merciful darkness had taken her.

Merciful darkness indeed. How naïve she had been.

The thing slapped closer, and for half a breath the moonlight illuminated a slick tentacle that was the color of swamp at midnight. When the tentacle graced the moonbeam, it bubbled and boiled and let out a squeal that made the Witch's ears ring.

She snatched up the bucket and focused her will upon the brittle edge. Trees had a long memory, and though this particular tree had never felt the embrace of a conflagration, all one had to do was to ignite the passion and kiss of heat. The Witch concentrated on the wood, remembering what it was like to hold a torch aloft with the flames dancing their waltz.

That was all it took.

The bucket blazed to life with blue fire, illuminating the room and casting the shadow into a chaotic frenzy. The tentacles, caught in the light, seized and shuddered upon the floor. Blisters broke out upon the creature's countless slimy appendages, and the room filled with a high-pitched mewl that drove the Witch to her knees.

The tentacles appeared to collapse in upon themselves, shrinking smaller and smaller. With a juicy pop, they exploded and covered the floor with a black ichor.

The Witch fell to the ground and scrambled until her back was against the wall. She was sure more of the things would come and kept the flame held out in front of her. Amazingly, the fire didn't eat the wood at all yet stayed ablaze, and so she sat until the sun rose and filled the room with natural light.

With the shadows banished to the darkest corners of the area, the Witch could relax. The room was familiar to her—it used to be the kitchen. It was here she experienced her final moments, brought low by a simple bucket of water.

She growled and kicked it against the wall. With the bucket out of the way, she noticed a pile of moth-eaten clothes and a pointy hat. Her hat. The Witch looked down and found nothing covering her pale skin. She was naked as the day she wriggled forth from her mother's greedy little womb.

The Witch took the clothes from the ground and shook the dust from them, causing an old black eye patch to fall from the bundle onto the floor. She put the clothes and hat on. The hat still fit perfectly, not that she expected any different. Once on, the stink of mildew and dust crawled up her nose.

"This won't do at all."

The Witch focused a mote of her will and snapped her fingers. The robes fluffed themselves, shaking the dust from them like they were a dog shaking water from its fur. Then, the blackness of the fabric turned blacker. The holes and tatters mended, and the stink turned into a nicer smell, one that reminded her of the forest in twilight.

"Much better."

There was one final thing. She leaned down, grabbed the old eye patch from the ground, and placed it on her head. With it on, she was complete once again.

With that taken care of, the Witch strode out of the room where she had so unceremoniously melted and made her way to a very special chamber. She navigated the halls and corridors without fail and knew she could do so blindfolded in the dark with her hands tied behind her back. However, the very thought of walking these halls in the dark made her shiver.

The Witch took a deep breath and centered herself. She would not let fear so easily conquer her. No, she would find out why she had returned to the realm of the living and what had happened to her castle.

Mighty oaken doors stood before her, nothing but shattered and splintered remnants of what they once were. The very sight of it stopped her in her tracks. If the doors were broken, then the crystal...

The Witch rushed into the chamber and screamed.

Her crystal ball was nothing more than broken shards and slivers of obsidian glass that covered the floor. She ran towards the ornate stone pedestal upon which the ball had once sat. The splinters of glass cut the bottoms of her feet, but she didn't care. The pain gave her something to focus on. It fueled her rage.

Surrounding the pedestal were four desiccated corpses wearing frayed robes of pale yellow. Their bodies lay in spots around the crystal ball corresponding to the four cardinal directions.

Clearly, they had been practitioners of the craft; however, she didn't recognize the robes, nor the strange symbols written in blood that stained their chests. The longer she stared at the symbols, the harder it became to focus on any details, and the Witch swore they shifted into different patterns when she looked away, even for a moment.

"Who were you, and what were you doing playing around with my tools?"

She walked past the blasted heap of bodies to the nearby window and gazed out at the craggy peaks that surrounded her castle. The path stretched out, and she knew it would connect to the Yellow Brick Road, and the road would take her to the Emerald City. Perhaps there that buffoon, Oz, could answer her questions.

With her mind set, the Witch strode out of the room. Yet the pop and crack of bone and the shuffle of feet across glass caused her to pause and turn around.

The four bodies stood upright, surrounding the pedestal. As one, their heads snapped towards her, and they all pointed out the window at the path. The Witch backpedaled out of the room, never taking her eye off the four robed figures. Something in her mind told her that to look away meant death.

Once they were out of sight, she exhaled. On her way out, she stopped at one of the supply closets. The Witch threw the bucket to the ground and retrieved a broom. It wasn't *her* trusted umbrella. No, that had been a focus for her power. The Witch knew she wouldn't be able to do as much with a broom, but hopefully, it would still serve her will in other ways. With her new weapon in hand, she hurried from the castle. It was no longer her home, and she was not welcome there.

After some time, the Witch came upon the Yellow Brick Road. However, the road wasn't as lustrous as before. Not that the Witch was complaining; she hated the dreadful yellow. The way it glistened in the sun and glittered. So brilliant and... happy. The road was different now.

It was repellant, almost revolting. The more the Witch thought about it, the more she decided it was unclean. That was the only word for it. As she stared at the road in front her, the color appeared to swirl in front of her eye. The movement made her head ache and made it difficult to breathe.

In the back of her mind, she saw twin suns setting on a lake of brackish water. A discordant melody burrowed into her ears, taking root before she could shake it off.

Then, as quick as it happened, it faded. The music echoed in the breeze until it was nothing more than a songbird's tune. The road stopped shifting and whispering until it was just a smoldering lane of blasted yellow. The Witch licked her lips and steeled her mind before setting foot on the damned road.

It wasn't long before the Witch found herself in the forest. While the land seemed different and out of place, there was a time, not too long ago (although she really didn't know how long she had been gone, so it may have been ages ago) that she found solace strolling through the trees. She had loved how they would watch her as she walked through them, muttering her machinations. However, now they didn't so much watch her as stare through her, as if she weren't even there to begin with. The trees themselves held blank expressions, lifeless. If it weren't for the yellow glow in their eyes, she would have sworn that the trees were dead.

With no other choice, the Witch continued. Soon, the sun began to set in the sky, but the way the last bit of its rays danced with the branches was odd. The shadows crawled at odd angles, angles that made her queasy. She glanced into the sky and gasped.

There wasn't just one sun.

There were two.

Twin suns blazed with a sickly yellow glow, painting the sky with a grotesque palette of reds and pinks that looked more like the viscera of a dead animal than anything else. The Witch took a few more steps, still staring at the horizon and the abysmal suns sinking low in the distance. She wasn't watching where she was going and ran into something cold, wet, and furry.

The Witch let out a scream and fell backward, landing hard in the dirt. In front her was a large creature, almost twice as tall as her. She scrambled away on all fours and snatched up her broom. With her wits about her once again, it only took a moment to ignite it and bathe the area in cool, blue firelight.

The creature in front her wasn't as tall as she had first thought. It was high in the air, but it was hanged from its neck. A length of hemp rope creaked and groaned as the body swayed from the Witch's impact.

The creature itself used to have golden brown fur, but it was so covered with matted blood, it was almost impossible to see. The Witch stood and brushed herself off. Then, with the non-burning end of the broom, she poked the creature to spin it around so she could get a good look at its face. Perhaps this was a bear, or a tiger, or... *oh my.*

The creature finally spun into view, and the Witch grimaced. It was Lion.

He was missing both eyes, leaving nothing more than bloody cavities. Someone (or something) had peeled Lion's lips away, leaving him forever snarling.

"Who did this to you?"

It was true that the Witch had once wanted to subjugate Lion and ride him. It would have amused her and added to her overall malice. She was wicked, but this was something else.

Pinpoints of milky gold glowed to life in Lion's eyes. He growled, a deep guttural growl that vibrated in the Witch's chest.

"You..." Lion said, although the word came out covered with writhing maggots.

The Witch took a step back and tried, unsuccessfully, to hide her trembling knees. She raised the broom as if it were one of the fearsome spears her Winkie Guards once carried.

Lion's eyes narrowed and he growled again. *"You should not be. You should not have come."*

"Speak not in riddles, or I will burn you," the Witch said and brandished her broom.

Lion laughed, though it was more of a wet croak filled with things that burrowed and things that whispered. "*I would welcome such a release.*"

"Who did this to you? Speak now!"

Lion champed his teeth at the Witch. "*I did. The play did. The black stars did...*" Lion looked to the sky and his jaw went slack. His body sagged as gravity pulled him always towards the ground. "*You should not be, Witch. You should not have come. Once you see it and witness it in all its infernal glory, you'll understand. You should not be, and now his hour is at hand.*"

"Who? Who is this mystery villain you speak of? No more nonsense!"

"*With both the East and West void of Witches, and when the Wizard departed Oz, it left a void. Something filled that void. Now, we are all servants of the King. Run while you can, or you will find yourself in the folds of his tattered robes.*"

The Witch narrowed her eyes and scowled at Lion. She waved him and his warning off. "Do not deem yourself worthy enough to cast orders at me. I go where I please, when I please, and I will meet this king you speak of, and he will pay for his transgressions."

With that, she walked past Lion and continued down the path. However, there came a snap, and another growl. The Witch whipped around and found only a frayed length of rope swaying in the breeze where once the Lion hanged.

She took a moment to compose herself before moving on.

As the Witch walked along the Yellow Brick Road, the air grew heavy and thick. It was a strange sensation, one she was not used to, nor one she particularly cared for. For it covered her in despair, making every movement and even the act of breathing difficult to complete.

It was the middle of the night when she came upon a dilapidated ramshackle structure of what once could have been a cabin in the woods.

The very forest itself had reclaimed the structure, as the roots of the trees burrowed through the windows like corpse-worms feasting on a bloated carcass. The Witch found a stump nearby and sat upon it for a moment of respite.

She peered into the sky, still amazed at the alien aspect of it all. These stars were not the same as she remembered. They were black things that burned with hatred and loathing as they crawled across the night's landscape. And the moons—the moons made her feel weak as they peered into her very wicked essence. The Witch shivered and pulled her robes tight about her chest.

The wind picked up and caused a paper to flutter, catching her attention. Nailed to the door, which had rotted away from one hinge and hung at a precarious angle, was a flier. Even from where she sat, the brilliant and decorative lettering scrawled across its length was visible.

She stood and ambled over to the house, now acutely aware of just how dark the interior of it was. As a precaution, she willed the flame to life on her broom once again, though it did little to fight the bleak gloom.

The flier continued to flutter, as if it were a trapped animal trying to get unstuck. The Witch used the broom's handle to pin it down so she could get a better look. It read:

Come and see
The King in Yellow
a play in two parts
one night only
The Royal Emerald Theater

The lettering was gilded in gold, printed on thick paper. There was more to the playbill; however, someone or something had ripped the bottom portion of the paper off.

"I saw it."

The Witch sucked in her breath and raised her broom defensively. The voice had come from inside the house. It was quiet and tinny.

"Reveal yourself!" The Witch demanded.

"I cannot."

More riddles. More games. The Witch had endured enough nonsense to last a lifetime. It was past time she made an example out of stubborn fools.

"If you cannot, then I shall. Behold, I am the Witch of the West!"

The Witch slammed the end of her broom onto the ground, and the earth shook beneath her. The battered door of the house blew to pieces as the blue flame flared brighter than the sun. Of course, it blinded her as well, but she hoped it made a statement.

Her eyesight returned quick enough, and the light from the flame pierced the shadows inside revealing a wooden chair. Upon the chair appeared to be a metal barrel of some sort.

"Who is there?" she asked.

"You shouldn't be," the voice said. It came from behind the chair.

"So I've been told."

The Witch strode into the house. Dead leaves crunched underneath her, cracking like thousands of tiny bones, as she picked her way closer to the chair. As she neared, the Witch circled around to the back side, ready to incinerate the unlucky fool who decided to test her. When she finally stepped around and saw who it was, she was at a loss for words.

The Tin Woodman's head dangled upside down, hanging onto his body in the chair by a thin shred of metal. His arms and legs were scattered to the four corners of the home. His eyes were gone, leaving empty holes in their place. Inside his chest were dozens of pieces of rotting meat. Upon further inspection, the Witch saw they were all human hearts.

"Tin Woodman..." the Witch said.

"I saw it," he said again. "I wish I never had. It was a terrible thing to undergo. The first act was nothing special, and I was going to leave. But as soon as the second act started, I could not. I saw it, and so will you. Though you should not be."

"The play?"

"I saw it. I saw it. I saw it. I saw it. I saw it. I saw it. I saw it. I saw it. I SAW IT I SAW IT I SAW IT ISAWITISAWITISAWIT..."

The walls appeared to close in on the Witch, and she couldn't breathe as the Tin Woodman continued to yell so loud and fast that she couldn't make out the words anymore. She ran from the house and tripped over a root in the doorway, falling to the ground. At the same moment, the Tin Woodman stopped speaking.

The Witch rolled to her side and peered back into the house. The Tin Woodman's body and head were gone, but the chair was still there. Draped across it was a robe made of tattered yellow cloth.

Something compelled her to stare at the cloth, and as she did, it moved ever so slightly. Whether it was the wind or something else that made that putrid cloth wriggle, she would never know, for she stepped out of the cabin and continued her journey down the Yellow Brick Road.

Her feet were covered in blisters, bleeding as she came to a great cornfield. Rows upon rows of dead, dried-out stalks yielding rotted husks of corn stretched on for longer than they should have. Crows and ravens circled above, and their caws filled the air with a chorus that was equal parts maddening and deafening.

She had no choice but to follow the road that cut through the field, and it wasn't long before she came across a scarecrow. After seeing what had happened to Lion and Tin Woodman, the Witch steeled herself, ready to confront whatever twisted monstrosity Scarecrow had become.

Yet, she wasn't ready for what came into view as she neared the figure.

It wasn't that idiot Scarecrow. It was a munchkin. Or rather, it had been a munchkin at one point. The Witch held no love for the munchkins, nor did they feel any love for her in return. However, she never would have wished this upon anyone.

The munchkin had once had curly blond hair; however, time and those creatures that prey upon carrion had taken their toll upon the munchkin's small form. Where rosy cheeks once had been was nothing more than sunblasted skin pulled tight across a skull. Stringy bits and strands of hair littered the munchkin's head, and its eyes had long ago become some bird's meal. Whoever did this had tied the munchkin up and secured his arms and legs with a length of hempen cord. The Witch walked past the poor thing and realized that whoever strung the munchkin up had also gutted him and replaced his insides with straw.

A piece of blood-stained paper was stapled to the munchkin's chest. It was another playbill for The King in Yellow. This one was intact and allowed the Witch to see what was on the bottom. It was a curious yellow symbol that resembled a three-sided question mark with three dots in the middle of it all. While she was familiar with sigils and glyphs, the Witch did not recognize this one, though it radiated with harrowing power.

The Witch balled her hand into a fist. Whoever did this would pay dearly, for Oz was her home. Wicked she may be, but nobody could destroy her realm and get away with it.

She turned to continue down the path and let out a gasp. Her gaze fell upon hundreds of munchkin scarecrows lining the Yellow Brick Road.

There was a faint pop from the munchkin next to her. The Witch turned and found the scarecrow was now pointing down the road towards Oz. A thunderous cracking noise boomed through the air as the rest of the munchkins followed suit, all pointing their lifeless fingers the same direction.

Towards answers.

The Witch set her chin and strode forward, hoping if anyone was watching, they wouldn't notice the tear on her cheek or the tremor in her steps.

The night dragged on longer than it should have. High above her, strange moons danced in the night sky with chaotic black stars that roiled with their own malevolent intent. They were like soulless eyes that gazed upon her with hunger.

Each step became harder than the next. By the time she crested the rise and the Emerald City appeared in the distance, the Witch could barely move. It was wrong. It was all wrong.

Before her wasn't the Emerald City at all. Some monstrous doppelganger had taken its place. Instead of the mighty towers (that only looked emerald if you wore those blasted green glasses that the buffoon, Oz, had created) that crested the horizon for all to see, twisted spires the color of tawny death replaced them. That city sat on the shore of a great lake that should not be...

You should not be.

...where only dry land once was. Yet, this city was not dead. Music played in the distance, a cacophonous, discordant noise, but still, it was music.

It pulled her closer. Begged her to come and listen. And she found herself wanting to listen. For there was something else in that music. Something she sought.

Answers.

The Witch stood upon bloodied feet, and putting one in front of the other, she made her way towards the dim city.

By the time she made it to the city gates, her feet were nothing more than bloodied meat. How she wished she had those silver slippers now. Yet, she persisted. She was the Witch of the West, was she not?

You should not be.

The gates were open and unguarded, but it would have mattered little, even if legions of soldiers guarded the walls. The Witch would not be stopped.

The streets were likewise empty of people; however, playbills for *The King in Yellow* littered the path and covered every square inch of wall. She followed the music until it became so loud it threatened to burst her eardrums.

When she finally came to her destination, the music stopped.

It led her to the Royal Emerald Theater, or rather, what used to be the Royal Emerald. The battered doors appeared broken from the inside as if a mob of patrons had busted free.

For a moment, the sounds of screams and growls flitted along the wind, but the noise disappeared as it had come.

The inside lobby looked like a great battle site. The furniture was in pieces, scattered across the room. The wallpaper was torn, and sections of the wall itself were missing, broken away, leaving behind jagged bits of splintered wood.

Standing at the threshold of the auditorium was Scarecrow. He had his back turned to the Witch, but she recognized his ratty clothing and ridiculous hat.

"You! Who did this?" she demanded.

Scarecrow stood silent but opened the door leading to the auditorium.

The Witch stood straight and walked towards Scarecrow. As she neared, he turned towards her.

He had no face.

In its place was a simple burlap bag. Blood stained the inside of the bag, and something pulsed on the inside.

"Who did this? Tell me!"

Scarecrow pointed to the auditorium. Inside, the seats were all empty except for three people sitting in the front row.

The Witch walked past Scarecrow towards the tiny audience. As she did, a spotlight turned on, illuminating the trio.

She knew them well, for they were her sisters. The Witch recognized Glinda's rich, red locks.

"Sisters! A sight for sore eyes. Tell me what is going on here!"

They did not answer. Scarecrow closed the door behind the Witch, and the auditorium was bathed in darkness apart from where her sisters sat.

The Witch's heart threatened to burst from her chest as the darkness embraced her. Just like before in her castle, there was something there with her. Something wet.

Something hungry.

The Witch willed her broom to light, and light it did, but its paltry blue flame did little to keep the shadows at bay. The pale glow flickered and shrank. The thing crashed into the seats behind her.

The Witch screamed and ran towards her sisters.

Whatever chased her was fast. The Witch channeled every bit of energy she had left into running. She was almost to the spotlight and her sisters when something cold and ropy wrapped around her waist. It tightened, blowing the air from her lungs and wrenching her into the dark.

When the Witch woke, she was in a chair. The first thing that came into view was Glinda's pink dress. She let out a sigh of relief and sat straight, turning towards her sister.

"Thank everything unnatural in this world, Glinda, what is—"

The Witch's words caught in her throat. She wanted to scream, but it wouldn't come.

Glinda was dead. No more than a dried husk, much like the corn in the cornfield—her face locked into an eternal scream of terror. What once was a beautiful, good Witch, was nothing more than a mummified shell, forever staring at the stage in terror.

The Witch leaned forward and found the other witches were the same.

Before she could rise and run for her life, the lights dimmed and the spotlight moved from the Witches to the stage.

A lone figure stepped onto the stage wearing a pallid yellow mask.

The orchestra struck an off-tune chord, chilling the Witch to the bone.

A presence loomed behind her. She dared not turn to look, but whatever it was, was ancient and powerful.

Tattered strips of yellow cloth fluttered in her periphery. She closed her eyes and looked away. Hands, as cold as the vast emptiness of space, gripped her cheeks and urged her to look on.

The play was about to start.

"THE GREAT JOINING"

There was a knock at the door.

Catherine looked at her watch. It was just past four in the afternoon and a little early for any trick-or-treaters. Besides, last year they only had one person come to the door and that was her husband Gerald's niece, Sylvie. Catherine wasn't surprised though. They lived far off the beaten track. Visitors were rare, even on Halloween. However, if the kids were going to put in the work to come all the way out to their cabin, she was going to reward them.

Catherine padded over to the kitchen counter and grabbed the bowl of full-sized candy bars before heading to the front door. When she opened the door, she expected to see Sylvie or at least some other kid in a costume. She didn't expect to see a grown man wearing purple sweatpants and nothing else.

He was older, with a bald pate and wispy hair the color of goose down. The man brought a shaky hand up to his face and rubbed his cheek.

Catherine wasn't sure what to do. Was this someone who was lost? The thick forest had swallowed its fair share of people throughout the ages. It was too easy to get lost in the tall trees.

"Can I help you?" Catherine asked.

The old man looked at her. His pupils were dilated, and his eyes were red. He opened his mouth, but no words came.

"Sir? Do you need help?"

He opened and closed his mouth, but still no sound. The man moved his hand from his cheek towards Catherine, and she took an instinctive step back. His claw-like fingers curled into a fist.

He whispered something.

Catherine didn't catch the words, but the sound made her skin crawl. There was something wrong with all of it. She wanted to slam the door in his face and lock it. There was something off with the man. However, he needed help.

"Can I call someone?"

The man whispered again and continued to whisper something over and over. She still couldn't quite hear him. Catherine moved closer and the words crawled into her ears.

"You should join us you should join us you should join us you should join us you should join us you should join us."

She was about to ask him what he was talking about, but movement at the edge of the property caught her eye. Two women walked up the driveway toward the cabin. Catherine let out a sigh of relief. They had to be looking for the old man. Perhaps they were relatives of his, or maybe they were caretakers. Catherine waved at them.

They didn't wave back.

As they neared, doubt burrowed into her mind. One woman wore an oversized t-shirt that had a cartoon panda on the front. It was something you would wear as pajamas, not for a stroll in the woods. The other wore a camouflaged Army uniform.

Deep down in her guts, Catherine knew they weren't wearing costumes. These weren't adults headed to a party or taking their kids out trick-or-treating. The way they walked toward the cabin was like a drunken shuffle.

The man reached out and grabbed her wrist.

Catherine let out a scream and dropped the bowl of candy. The glass shattered, sending dozens of shards in all directions.

He pulled her close enough that his rancid breath was hot in her face.

"You should join us."

Catherine pulled her arm free and pushed the man with all her strength. He stumbled backward and lost his footing on their porch steps. The man fell and hit the ground hard with a crack.

Catherine stood in the doorway in shock. She hadn't meant to push him so hard. It was a reaction. Self-preservation. Still, she may have just killed the old man. Her stomach twisted into knots and bile rose in her throat. Catherine took a step towards him. He wasn't moving.

"Oh my god, oh my god, oh my god."

He sat up, and Catherine yelped. The old man got up off the ground. She let out a sigh of relief, thankful she hadn't killed him.

"Sir, are you okay? I'm so sorry, I didn't mean to—"

His arm was broken. Bad.

His forearm had a bloody gash with a white shard of bone sticking out of it. Blood poured from the wound and splattered onto the dirt beneath the old man's feet.

He looked at her and stepped back up onto the porch.

"You should join us."

The two women came up behind him and climbed onto the porch as well. They all stared at her with the same blank expression.

"You should join us," they said in unison.

Catherine slammed the door shut and locked it.

The mass of people outside of Catherine's house had grown into a small horde. They kept arriving, one after another. Sometimes they showed up alone, at other times, groups of them came walking from the forest that bordered her property.

She had tried calling the police, but the lines were busy. How were the lines busy for emergency services? It didn't make any sense at all. Catherine kept hoping it was all some horrible nightmare or a stupid Halloween stunt. That the host of that show, *Scared Stupid,* would come walking out to let her know she was on camera, and she'd been duped. But as more and more people showed up, that hope dwindled.

Catherine ran from room to room, double checking each door and window. They were all locked. She had turned off all the lights in the house and stayed as quiet as possible. Hopefully, they would move on and leave her alone, though as Gerald had always said, hope wasn't a good plan of action.

Catherine pulled her phone out and called him. It rang a few times then went to his voicemail just like the dozens of other times she had tried. Instead of leaving him a message, she sent him a text.

There are tons of people outside of the house. I don't know what they want. They are all just standing there.

She crept to the window and peeked through the blinds. There were more people than before. They stood there staring at the house.

Her phone buzzed in her pocket, and she let out a yelp before covering her mouth. Catherine scrambled away from the window until she touched the wall of the living room. As she slid to the floor, she grabbed her phone. Gerald had returned her text.

Don't go outside! Stay put. I'm on my way home. It's crazy out here.

The boards of the porch outside creaked, and Catherine's heart skipped a beat. Several silhouettes moved across the window.

More and more footsteps strained the aging wood of her porch, as more and more people crowded up against the house. How would Gerald even get in with all those people out there? The short answer: he wouldn't.

There was a knock at the door, just three taps.

Catherine shook her head and hugged her legs. This wasn't happening. It couldn't be happening.

There was another knock, three more taps.

"Go away. Go away... please."

The knocks continued. This time, instead of just three, they kept going. The knocks were almost robotic in their rhythm, like a metronome.

Catherine crawled towards the door and the knocking stopped. She held her breath.

"Come outside and join us."

It was a woman's voice. Probably older from the lower pitch and gravelly sound.

Catherine stood on shaky legs and peered out the peephole. It was indeed an older woman with long white hair. She wore a dirty nightgown and no shoes. It couldn't have been more than 50 degrees outside. How the woman wasn't shivering in the cold didn't make sense. The woman stared at the peephole, and Catherine had the sense that the woman could see her.

"Come outside and join us," the old woman said. She cocked her head to the side and smiled.

Catherine backed away from the door as she fished her phone from her pocket. The knocking started again.

She called 911 again. It *actually* rang this time! After three rings, a dispatcher answered.

"911, what is your emergency?" asked a male voice from the other side of the call.

"There is a large group of people on my property who refuse to leave. I'm scared they are going to break in," Catherine said.

"Is anyone trying to get in at the moment, ma'am?"

"No, not yet. But there are so many! Please send some cops! My husband is on his way home!"

"Please calm down, ma'am. There's no need to panic."

No need to panic? This wasn't just a couple of teenagers pulling Halloween pranks.

"Just send some police, quick!"

"Don't worry. They'll come for you. But I need you to do something for me, okay?"

"What do you need? Please hurry," Catherine said.

"I need you to go outside and join them."

Catherine's breath caught in her throat. "What?"

"Ma'am, I need you to go outside and join them."

Catherine screamed and ended the call. The knocking continued. Catherine ran upstairs and looked out the window. There were more people gathered outside than ever before. She ran to another room and looked out. The people surrounded the house. They all looked up in unison at her, heads cocked to the side with grins stretched across their faces.

Catherine's phone buzzed. It was a message from Gerald.

Almost there. Just pulling up now.

Tears streamed down Catherine's face as she hammered a message back.

They are all out there! Be careful, and if they try to get you, run!

Gerald pulled into the dirt lane that led to their house. The headlights from the truck washed over the crowd standing in the yard. The people didn't pay him any mind but instead continued to stare up at Catherine from below. The truck shut off, and the lights went out. Catherine watched and waited, but nothing happened. Gerald stayed in the truck. Then, her phone buzzed again.

I'm going to make a run for it. Get ready to open the door when I get there.

Catherine's heart was racing. A thousand thoughts shot through her mind, playing out all different scenarios—none of them ending well for Gerald.

No! Don't do it!

It was too late. Gerald got out of the truck and started to barrel his way through the crowd. Catherine watched in horror as he pushed his way through. The people didn't react to him, instead continuing to stare up at her. She didn't want to look away, but at the same time, she had to get back downstairs and get ready to open the door.

Catherine ran, taking the stairs three at a time. She lost her footing halfway through and tumbled down. Pain lanced through her hip as she rolled, and something cracked in her leg. She let out a cry of agony and fought back the urge to vomit. When she tried to stand, something gave in her leg, and she crumpled back to the ground.

There was a knock at the door. This time it was different. It wasn't the rhythmic knocking from before but instead a desperate slamming.

"Let me in!"

It was Gerald!

Catherine crawled toward the door as fast as she could. Each movement sent spikes of agony piercing through her body. She cried out but kept crawling. Gerald needed her. Depended on her. She wouldn't let him down.

The jingle of keys came from outside followed by the tell-tale fumble of someone trying to work the deadbolt. As she neared the door, the lock unlatched. Gerald came in and slammed the door behind him, breathing heavily.

He turned and his eyes went wide when he saw Catherine on the floor.

"Oh my god, are you okay?" he asked.

Gerald knelt and scooped her up in his arms. It hurt as he jostled her into an embrace, but she melted into him.

"What's happening? Why are they all out there?" Catherine asked.

Gerald let go of the hug and cupped Catherine's face in his hands. He smiled at her.

"I don't know, honey. I really don't. But I think you should come outside and join us."

"Rocky Mountain Hocus"

L ehi, Utah 1948

I've never liked dead bodies. They don't shut up. I'd suggest not listening to whatever it is they have to say. They will drive you insane, tell you lies, or try to trick you into doing something your mama wouldn't approve of. They're not your loved ones or friends anymore. The simple fact of the matter is, once someone dies and their soul departs, it leaves a void. Sometimes, things like to crawl into that void. This particular dead body liked to lie, and it was very chatty, which made it hard to concentrate.

I knew them as skinners—lowly critters that liked to wear human bodies like clothes.

I clutched the medicine bag that hung around my neck. As soon as I did, the thing's voice fell away in a buzz and I could think straight. The rest of the world came into focus, and I let out the lungful of air I'd been holding. This medicine bag was a godsend, a gift from a friend of mine in the war. His name was Two Feathers. He found me in the med-tent about to lose my mind because one of those things had crawled into the dead man in the bed next to me. Needless to say, the medicine bag made day-to-day business bearable.

The medicine bag became hot in my hand, hotter than my granddad's wood burning stove in December. I let it fall to my chest.

"Nice try, cowboy. Didn't your mama tell you it's rude to ignore your elders?"

I ignored it. Talking to it wouldn't do anyone any good.

"We should ask your mama. She's in Hell doing some awful nasty things."

More lies. I took a deep breath and tried to focus on the scene. I was looking for Herman West, a local carpenter and known chicken fighter in the area. He'd been missing, presumed dead, and I was supposed to find him. Finding dead bodies wasn't a fun business, but I was good at it.

It was dark in the beat-up coop, and dusty. Chicken shit littered the dirt floor like a nasty rug, and it didn't smell very nice either. The lone rooster in the coop kept its distance from me but continued to feed as it strutted about. Its feet were dark in color, probably one of those Blackfeet birds of Mr. Lewis. Supposedly, they were good fighting birds. Whoever killed West wasn't interested in the prize fighter.

"She's down here with your platoon. They're having a grand ol' time."

My feet stuttered as my heart skipped a beat. Shouldn't have listened to it.

The rooster cast me a sidelong glance and then went back to scratching for bugs in the dirt. The familiar blast of M-1 shots and grenades rattled in the back of my mind. But that sound wasn't here. It wasn't now. I tried to regulate my breathing and then got back to work.

All in all, it looked like a normal chicken pen, with the exception of the small bit of finger sticking out of the earth. If I were a betting man, I'd say that hand belonged to Mr. West. Looked like the skinner calling West home wasn't too strong, otherwise it would have walked out of here by now. It was going to be one of those weeks.

I let out a sigh and walked out of the coop.

"Where the hell you think you're going? We ain't done talking, cowboy! You know it's only a matter of time before you join the chorus, don't you?"

The thing's voice faded as I walked out and into the sunlight. The clucks and crows of the roosters in the yard filled the air with a kind of music I usually found enjoyable. At the moment, it just added to my headache.

I was almost to my truck when Albert West came running up to me. His face was red, and he was taking in big gulps of air. The kid needed to lay off the sweets.

"Did you find my pa, mister?"

I rubbed the back of my neck and avoided his gaze.

"Better call the police, son. Your father's buried in the coop."

No better way than the blunt way. That's what my father used to say. I got into the truck and fired it up. The '41 Chevy roared to life.

Albert stood in the road staring off into the distance. I figured it would be best to get along before he decided to ask questions. I shifted the truck into first and drove around him. I left him, the roosters, and the body behind in a plume of dust and smoke.

"Buried in the coop, eh?" Brutus asked.

I took a sip of coffee and nodded. The coffee was hot, and burned a little as it went down, but it warmed my soul. Brutus hadn't touched his drink since I told him about West. He hadn't flinched or reacted much. He must have expected the news.

"What are you going to do now, Warwick?" Brutus asked.

"Hit the road. The rodeo in Reno starts in a couple days. There's a bull with my name on it."

I finished my coffee and grabbed my hat. Brutus held a hand up and motioned for me to stop. Here it was, the moment I knew was coming.

"Can you find out who killed him?" he asked.

I let my hat fall back onto the table and grabbed a cigarette from my coat pocket.

"I need to hit the road. I was only supposed to be here for a couple of nights."

"I know, I know. I wouldn't ask if it weren't important. Besides, you have a knack for this kind of work."

"What's it to you anyway? Were you and West friends?"

"We served together at Midway. You were at Guadalcanal, weren't you?"

If I could go the rest of my life without hearing that word again, I'd die a happy man. My palms started to sweat. A small cough escaped my lungs as the waitress walked by with more coffee. I caught her eye and nodded to my cup. She shot me a cheap smile and filled the mug with even cheaper coffee.

After the waitress walked away, Brutus took an envelope out of his coat pocket and pushed it across the table. Payment for finding West.

I grabbed it and stuffed it into my own pocket. No need to count the money; Brutus had never cheated me.

"I don't like doing this kind of work," I said.

"I know, but you're damn good at it. Besides, I owe it to West. He saved my life once," Brutus said.

I sighed and sipped my coffee. Brutus knew what buttons to push. He always had.

"When's the next derby?"

"Tomorrow night at Young's farm."

I finished the coffee and relished the burn. Brutus wore an empty smile on his face. Something was going on. I guess he figured I would find out what that something was. Without a word, I grabbed my hat and walked out of the diner.

There were a lot of people at the farm. Three rows of cars and trucks lined up near the Young's two-story home. I parked my rig and grabbed the .45 from the glove box. It never hurt to be prepared.

With the gun tucked away in my waistband, I stepped out into the crisp night air. Laughter and talk drifted from the barn nearby. It was an old rickety structure that a mouse's fart could tip over.

I threw my jacket on and headed toward the noise. Gravel crackled underneath my boots, and for a split second, the Utah farmland melted away. The familiar smell of jungle humidity mixed with blood flooded my senses. The buzz of a Zero flew overhead, and I fought the urge to take cover. I clutched the medicine bag with a death grip, focusing on the act of breathing as the jungles of Guadalcanal faded into memory, replaced by the reality of the farm.

"You okay, sir?"

I opened my eyes. A young lady with curly hair the color of strawberries stood in front of me.

"Yes, ma'am. Just a little upset stomach is all."

Red shot me a look that said she didn't believe an ounce of my bullshit. That was fine.

"It will be a dollar please. Entry fee and all," Red said.

"A dollar? You have to be kidding me."

"'Fraid not, mister. That's what my pa said. Dollar from everyone. Unless you're fighting in the derby or want to join a hack fight, then it's more."

I dug a dollar out of my wallet and handed it over.

"No, ma'am. I'm just here to watch."

She shot me a smile and pocketed the bill. I went to step past her, but she stopped me.

"A couple of rules first."

I raised an eyebrow. Red extended a hand with her thumb and two fingers splayed.

"One," she tucked her thumb away. "No drinking. If we catch you drinking, you'll be asked to leave." She tucked her index finger away. "Two, no fighting. We catch you starting something like that, and we'll ask you to leave, but not nicely." There was a wicked glint in her eyes as she finished. "And three, have fun."

I tipped my hat towards her and walked past. The barn came alive with a mixture of cheers, disappointment, and excitement—a mix usually only found in shady establishments such as this. I couldn't help but jump on that wagon and ride along with everyone else.

Makeshift seating made from bales of hay circled the fighting pit. A man wearing a worn leather jacket walked away with a dying rooster in his hands. Another fellow with large, thick glasses pumped his arm in the air and shook hands with the referee.

I scanned the crowd. Brutus sat near the pit with a wad of cash in his hand. He caught my eye for just a moment before he looked away with a slight nod to his side. A couple of goons stood near the wall guarding a door. Judging from their size, they were corn fed and never missed a meal.

I made my way towards the two. One of the thugs shot me a look that would sour milk. He didn't say anything, just glared. The other smiled—the kind of smile the devil makes when he strikes a deal.

"Can I help you, sir?" Smiley asked.

"I was hoping I could get back there. The knife fights, I reckon?" I asked.

"Are you expected?"

I reached into my coat pocket. Sour Milk tensed, but Smiley just kept grinning. He was definitely the dangerous one. I pulled out a roll of bills and showed it to the both of them.

"Nope, but I don't think it's a problem, is it?" I asked.

Smiley kept his eyes locked to mine. He nodded, and Sour Milk opened the door.

"Good luck, sir."

I tipped my hat and walked past them. I'd be sure to charge that expense to Brutus.

The room was dark. Cigarette smoke slid across what little lighting there was. Unlike the other area, this place was quiet. A dozen people sat in folding chairs watching the match.

It wasn't so much the change of attitude that put me on edge. It was the fact that my medicine bag heated up. Nobody turned to look my way, but all eyes were on me.

If I wasn't doing this for Brutus, I would have turned around and walked away right then and there. However, friendship was a funny thing that had gotten me into trouble more times than I could count.

I found an empty chair and took a seat. A tall man with a widow's peak puffed on a corn-cob pipe in the center of the pit. He stepped out of the gloom and stood under a bare light bulb.

"Bill 'em up!" he said. His voice vibrated the medicine bag and rasped against my soul. Kind of made me sick to my stomach.

I was in over my head.

Two handlers stepped forward and held their roosters close to one another. The birds started to peck at each other. The display went on while another man with a cane walked by each member of the audience. He got to me.

"Take your bet, sir?" the man asked.

"I'll sit this one out, thanks."

He nodded and walked off. I was grateful I had grabbed my gun before I left the truck.

"Put 'em on the line, boys. Let's get this dance started," the referee said. Again, hearing him talk churned my insides. The medicine bag heated up even more. My breathing picked up, and for a moment the room went blurry. I needed to leave. The two goons came in from outside as if they'd heard me and posted on the door. So much for that plan.

The handlers put their roosters on the far line.

"Pit!" the referee said. The call sent my ears ringing.

The roosters in the pit jumped into the air and kicked up dust and feathers. The dull light bounced off the razors that replaced their spurs, creating a dazzling effect.

They collided into one another in a violent clash. It was nature perverted. I didn't mind a regular fight, but a knife fight was something else. Something brutal. It pulled at strings inside me that played a discordant song; only, after a bit, the song started to sound good. That's what scared me the most.

It didn't take long. One bird was dead, the other dying. Without a sound or applause, the crowd stood, collected their winnings, then filed out. I kept my seat and waited. What was about to happen didn't require an audience.

"Took a lot of guts to come here, cowboy," the referee said. Something scratched the insides of my skull as he spoke. He lit his pipe. For a split second, the flare of his match showed his face. Alabaster skin drooped from the man's bones like a sick mask. I wanted to scream, but it wouldn't help. Trust me, I tried once, and all I got for my trouble was not being able to talk for a week.

I gripped the medicine bag, which helped. Not much, but a little was more than enough to find my courage.

"Well, I figured it was bad when I found Mr. West," I said. "Couldn't be just one of you skinners around here."

"Mr. West... didn't live up to our expectations."

"Neat."

I reached for the gun with my free hand. Corncob took a long drag on his pipe and waved an arthritic hand. The medicine bag burst into flames. I let out a growl as I ripped it from my neck.

As soon as it left my body, voices came alive all around me. A chorus of dozens screamed, pleaded, and cried. It was a choir of men, women, children, and other things a man wasn't supposed to hear. I fell to my knees and covered my ears, but it was no use. The voices burrowed deep inside, cracking the shell of my psyche—not that it was that hard of a shell. Corncob's slick words cut through all of them.

"We've been waiting a long time for you, Warwick."

The lights dimmed as Corncob's smoke filled the room. The silence was blasted away by the buzz of machine-gun fire. I broke out in a cold sweat. I wanted to run far and hide, but I just couldn't. Screams crept through the darkness ahead of me. I recognized the voices.

I was in the jungle again.

"Cowboy! You still there? Help!"

The cry came from the other side of the trees, cutting through the air. After a moment, I could move, although I didn't want to. I'd seen what lay through the trees a million times over.

The scene melted away as I emptied the Colt into the center of the fighting pit. Corncob wasn't there anymore, just a trail of pipe-smoke.

His laughter slithered from the corner. Somehow, I got to my feet and turned to the door. Corncob was right in front of me. He grinned. The smile was too large for any human's face to handle. He blew a mouthful of smoke into my eyes, and everything went dark.

I woke in the center of the pit. The crowd had taken their seats and watched like a pack of hungry dogs waiting for a bone. Corncob straddled my chest. He still had his pipe tucked into the corner of his mouth. Black smoke poured from the cob bowl. His eyes smoldered with each puff.

"Well, looks like it's the end of the road for you, cowboy."

I didn't respond. What was the point?

"Sorry," a familiar voice said.

I turned my head. Brutus stood in the corner. Smiley and Sour Milk stood on either side of him. He couldn't look me in the eye.

"You too?" I asked.

"I'm sorry, I didn't have a choice," Brutus said.

It all made sense now. The knowing expressions, the manipulation. All a ploy to get me here.

"Our dear Brutus knows how to live up to expectations," Corncob answered.

I tried to shake him off my chest, but he slammed me back into the dirt. Corncob's grip was strong. Stronger than any skinner I'd ever encountered.

I kept struggling though—Mama didn't raise quitters. Pain lanced through my hand as I felt through the dirt, and I instinctively pulled away. The light flashed off something metallic on the ground. I grabbed for it, picking up a discarded razor from one of the fights.

"Now it's time for you to join the chorus, Warwick."

Corncob grabbed my head and slammed it into the earth. Stars flashed in my vision as the room spun upon impact. Everything went squirrelly. I wanted to sleep and let it all slip away, but the razor in my hand kept me anchored. He leaned in close.

"This won't hurt a bit," he said.

Liar.

Corncob took a deep drag on his pipe. That black smoke slipped out of the corners of his mouth as if it were alive and fighting to get out. Before he could blow it all out, I swiped up with the razor, cutting him across his throat.

The smoke burst from the wound, and Corncob fell off me. He was kicking in the dirt and let out a screech that would have put a crow to shame. Everyone bolted for the door as the light disappeared. Smoke spun through the room like a tornado, and a thousand voices screamed out. One voice stood out.

I think it was my mama's.

I woke up to a world of hurt. I hadn't felt this way since I tried to ride that big brahma bull in Billings. The room was empty, chairs were overturned, and the door hung on one hinge. Corncob was gone. Just his pipe lay in the dirt. There was no sign of his goons. No idea why they hadn't jumped me. Perhaps I had a guardian angel watching over me. More than likely with Corncob getting stuck like he did, they chose to run while they had the chance. I was grateful either way.

My medicine bag was in the dirt next to me, charred but still somewhat intact. When I grabbed it, my headache dulled, and some of the background voices quieted to a whisper. Still worked despite being burned. Not as good though. I'd have to find me a medicine man.

I was pretty sure that skinner was still out there somewhere. It was probably searching for another corpse to call home. That meant I had some time before it came after me.

I shuffled my way out into the barn. Everything hurt as I limped toward the truck. I hoped a nice hot cup of coffee would take the edge off. I had to get to Reno. There was a bull with my name on it.

"Dead Man's Hand"

I took a seat in the corner of the Billy Brock's Saloon, making damn sure my back was toward the wall. I had already been shot once today, and I wasn't looking to get bushwhacked while I was bending an elbow or playing cards.

The saloon was a small hole-in-the-wall building with an actual hole in the wall. Dust covered everything no matter how much Billy tried to keep the place in order. I reckon it was due to the endless sea of dirt and sage just outside the walls.

I didn't much like the place, but it was familiar, and familiar was what I needed. I'd played cards many times in Billy's establishment, hustling anyone willing to gamble with me. I was good at poker, but I was better at ensuring I'd win. Sometimes you had to lose a bit, get the other players comfortable, and then spring the trap.

The sun blasted everything outside in an unbearable heat, which made everything inside stuffy. I wanted to take my coat off but wasn't about to advertise the fact that I had been shot.

"Hey there, Jack, what'll it be?" Billy asked.

"The usual."

There weren't many folks in the saloon, just the usual drunks and miners looking for a watering hole or a poke at one of the girls in the *establishment* across the way. I didn't mind it none. Some peace and quiet would do me good, along with some spirits.

Billy returned with a bottle of cheap whiskey and a grimy glass that had seen better days. I reached for the bottle, and pain shot up my side, causing a grunt to escape my lips. I wasn't a medicine man, but I was pretty sure I was dying. I told that idiot with the scattergun to keep it trained on the passengers, but he was a curious sort, and I got winged because of his lack of focus. Could have been worse I suppose, 'cause he got dead.

Someone was tickling the ivories on Billy's old piano, filling the room with a tune. It was a soft melody, but it scratched the back of my mind as if I'd heard it before. I couldn't quite place it and gave up trying.

The whiskey burned as it slid down my throat; it was a good burn. Two more followed suit, and then I gave it a rest, hoping it would take the edge off the lead stuck in my chest. My pa used to tell me, "Hope in one hand and shit in the other and see which will fill up faster." He was a smart man, and I was a stubborn fool.

The music stopped, and the man who had been playing sauntered over to my table. A blood-red bandana was wrapped around his head, keeping a heap of wheat-colored hair at bay. I kept one hand on my pistol just under the table in case he wanted to try and put the final nail in the coffin.

"Leave me be, stranger."

He flashed me a smile colder than a January morning in the high mountains. Could have been the blood loss, but I swear something flashed behind his eyes. Just a flicker of movement beneath the surface as if his face were a mask.

"You've been a naughty boy, Jack."

The stranger's voice slithered through the air, a cat on the prowl looking for some unsuspecting prey. It made my skin want to crawl off my bones and hide in a dark corner.

"Is that so? And what makes you think you know a damn thing about me?"

I pulled the hammer back on my pistol, trying to move it slow enough not to make a noise, but when it clicked into place, firing it would have been the only thing louder.

The strange man smiled a crooked smile and took a seat in one of the empty chairs. He drummed his fingers on the table, his long and pointed fingernails leaving small scratches in the old wood.

"What do you want?"

The question caused a coughing fit to rise in my chest, sending waves of pain rolling through my body. Something wet was making its way up my throat, and I put a hand in front of my mouth to stop it from flying out. The bloody phlegm I hocked up was a bad sign.

"I want you, Jack. You're dying, and I've come to collect."

I returned the smile and pulled the trigger on my pistol. I was expecting to gut shot the stranger sitting in front of me. What I wasn't expecting was a misfire. The man smiled even wider and sat back in his chair. I jerked the gun up above the table and pulled the trigger three more times, each one producing nothing but a dull click.

"Who are you?"

"I go by many names, but you can call me Sam."

"Sam, you old goat, how do you know we don't want him?" A new voice boomed from the bar, shaking the walls of the saloon and spilling dust from the rafters. Sam sneered. He refused to look back at the speaker and instead poured himself a drink from my bottle of whiskey.

The man walked over from the bar, taking a seat next to Sam. He was an older gentleman with a long beard that had seen better days and eyes grayer than granite. Like Sam, something seemed to move behind those eyes, something old.

"Who the hell are you and what do you want?' I asked, taking my drink back from Sam, which elicited a sneer from the man.

"I'm nobody really, but you can call me Pete. I'm here to save you from damnation."

The old timer didn't look the part of one of those sin-busters thumping on their good books and preaching about salvation, but who was I to judge? There was a familiarity to the old man, as if I'd known him for a long time. There was also an overwhelming sense of disappointment rolling off him.

"Jack, he's right," Pete said, pointing to Sam. "You have sinned. Right now, your fate could go either way. Up or down."

"Nah, he's damned and he knows it. Too many sins to count if you ask me."

Sam was grinning again, and this time there was a bit of warmth coming off his smile. It wasn't a pleasant kind of warmth either.

"Get the hell out of here and leave me be. Let me get soaked in peace!"

I unloaded the dud bullets from my pistol and was about to reload when the saloon went completely dark save for a small circle of orange light above the table. All the sounds of breathing, shuffling glasses, and murmurs ceased to exist, leaving nothing but silence to echo throughout the room. Sam and the old man stared at me, not speaking.

"What is this?"

"It's your death, Jack. You'll be dead in less than hour. The bullet clipped something important in that poor excuse of a body you have and you're bleeding out. I'm sorry," Pete said.

"Yep, you'll be belly up in the boot hill before morning," Sam said with a chuckle.

I believed them. The slow trickle of blood and the sinking feeling in my guts verified it. I finished off the bottle of whiskey, happy that the pain in my chest had finally dulled.

"Well, isn't that swell? So what happens now?"

"We figure out where you're going to go. You're coming with one of us."

"More than likely you're coming with me. I've got a lot of fun things planned, Jack. Things you'll enjoy," Sam said.

The orange light above the table flared at the end of Sam's sentence and set ghost lights dancing in front of my eyes for a moment. The smell of rotten eggs smacked my face, and I almost lost all the wonderful whiskey I'd drank.

"That's enough," Pete said.

At his command, the orange light softened until it was replaced by a glowing blue orb. The pain my chest faded, which was nice, as did the buzz of the whiskey, which wasn't nice.

"The problem is that you've tip-toed the line, Jack. It could really go either way," Sam said. "Which brings us to the here and now."

Sam drummed his fingers on the table again, his face locked in that fake grin that fit him like a tailored suit.

I didn't like where this was going, and I needed to stall, buy some time. That's when it hit me.

"Well, I tell you what, how about we play a few hands before I go?" I asked. "Doesn't seem like either of you are in a rush."

Sam scratched his chin and then clasped his hands together.

"Why the hell not?" Sam said.

"It will only delay the inevitable, Jack," Pete said.

"I've played cards here hundreds of times. It would be nice to play another round before I go."

"Very well."

A deck of cards appeared on the table from out of nowhere. There wasn't a poof or a pop. They simply were there when moments before they were not. I picked them up and they were familiar, as if I had played with them for years.

The cards shuffled as natural as a waterfall and slicker than hot grease on a fry pan. I cut the deck with one hand and shuffled them again with a smile creeping into the corner of my lips.

"Okay boys, here it is: five-card draw, let's play a few."

Sam scooted his chair up closer to the table. "We need some music."

He snapped his fingers, causing a spark to flash as if he'd just hit steel against flint. Somewhere in the darkness, a fiddle started to play. The music was chaotic, manic, and rushed, but buried deep within the discord was something catchy.

Pete sighed and scooted up to the table as well. He snapped his fingers and Sam's fiddle playing stopped, replaced by a typical piano tune. He nodded toward the cards, his eyes warm and kind.

I played the first hand watching. Observing. The old timer didn't move a muscle in his face the entire time. No twitch, no smile, hell, not even a frown. Just a deadpan glare at the cards in front him, as if he were sleeping. I'd almost given up hope that I'd be able to read him when the corner of his eye shifted. There it was.

He won that hand, eliciting a round of cursing from Sam. Many of the words I was intimately familiar with. Others, well, I couldn't even tell what language they were in. I may have lost the round, but I'd gained some potentially priceless knowledge.

The next round, Sam won. He had so many tells that it was hard to pick which one was authentic and which one was bullshit. He was going to be a bigger challenge.

We played probably a dozen hands. The whole time I watched the two men. Verifying tells and forcing situations on the other two. It was hard to focus, given that I was supposed to be dying and going to heaven or hell, but I tried.

I shuffled the deck a few times, the cards now an extension of my hands. After the right amount, I moved the deck toward Pete.

"What's wrong? I'm not good enough to cut the deck?" Sam asked, placing his hand across his chest and casting a frown that belonged on a stage my way.

"I don't trust you."

"Moi?"

Pete tapped the top of the deck and pushed them back my way. Bold move. His mistake.

I smiled and dealt the cards out. The entire time, Sam drummed his fingers, louder and louder, never breaking eye contact with me.

"You know, you're already dead. You've bled out and you're lying face down on that grimy table in good old Billy Brock's saloon."

Trying not to listen to Sam was like trying not to breathe. As each moment thundered on, it was harder and harder to endure.

"Face down, blood pooling at your boots. Hell, you might have already shit your pants by now. You've seen enough dead bodies to know that happens."

I hesitated dealing the last round of cards. I put the deck down and rubbed my temples.

"Before we end this, can I get a drink?" I asked.

"Sure thing, Jack. For you, anything."

Sam snapped his fingers, causing the sparks to fly through the air once again. This time though, a puff of smoke appeared over the table. When the smoke cleared, a bottle of whiskey sat in its place. He poured me a shot and placed it in front of me.

To say I'd drank a lot in my years would be like saying it was cold in the Dakota Territory, both true, but understatements. It didn't just get *cold* in the Dakota Territory, it got colder than a witch's tit in a snowstorm cold. Needless to say, I knew my whiskeys, which was why I was surprised when I drank what was in my glass. I'd never, in any of my outlawin' years, tasted a whiskey like that. It burned hotter than a midsummer's day in Texas, searing my throat the whole way down. Yet it was good. There was a smokiness to it that I'd never tasted before mixed with a spice that had my tongue begging for more. It reminded me of the time I'd bedded that little Mexican rose near the border. She was wild, full of life, and full of sin.

"What in the hell is that?"

"Not many have had my own special cask. Consider yourself lucky."

"Bah, devil piss and nothing else," Pete said. He poured a shot from a silver flask he had stashed away in his coat pocket. "Try this."

I sipped it, unsure of what to expect. Instead of a burn, it was mellow, smooth, and complex. It was the moment before the sun rose above the mountains, that quiet time that you know you should get moving, but you can't because you're lost in all those colors marching through the s ky.

"Devil piss? It's better than that fluffy juice you call a drink."

My stomach was happy again, warm and radiant. While they were bickering about whose whiskey was better, I picked up the deck and dealt the last round of cards, sliding a card off the bottom when I came to my pile.

I watched as they picked up their cards, looking for the tells I had identified. Satisfied with what they were showing me, I felt confident with my next move.

"How about we make this interesting?" I said.

"You mean playing cards with me isn't interesting enough?" Sam asked.

"What exactly are you getting at?" Pete asked.

"If smiley here wins, then I guess I'm going to the lake of fire, and if you win, then you can take me to the great range in the sky."

"And if you win?" the old timer asked.

"Glad you asked... If I win, then you leave me be and let me get on my own way. Neither of you takes me anywhere."

Pete arched one of his eyebrows while Sam laughed and slapped his knee.

"Now you're playing with fire. I love it!" Sam said.

"You would gamble your eternal soul?" Pete asked.

"Better than you two bastards deciding for me."

"Done! But we're playing stud this time. Let Fate decide what's going to happen," Sam said, slapping the table. The floor shook from the blow and rattled my teeth.

"Are you sure?" The old timer asked, his eyes heavy with concern.

"Yes, indeed. Let's do this."

"Okay, Jack. You are free to make your own choices. Done."

The room vibrated again. It wasn't as strong as when Sam had slapped the table, but it was no less noticeable.

I grabbed my cards. Two Aces, two Eights, and a King to round it all out. I did my best to hide my disappointment. It wasn't a bad hand, but I was hoping for something more. My soul was on the line. Something had gone wrong. Perhaps I had missed a card in the shuffle, or maybe I counted wrong.

Pete gave me a heavy look, his eyes full of sorrow. With a small shake of his head, he put his cards on the table.

"Fold."

I raised an eyebrow, keeping all other emotion off my face. Then, I turned my attention back to Sam. Pete's gaze bore through me like a Bowie knife, cutting through my soul. I tried my best to push it out of my mind.

"Really? You're going to fold? You know we aren't up-ping the ante at all. You could just play and see how the cards drop," Sam said with a half sneer.

"I've lost," was all Pete said.

"How about you, what have you got?" I asked.

Sam placed his cards on the table, splayed out in a perfect fan. He sat back in his chair, placing his hands behind his head.

"You know what, Jack? I like you. I feel like if circum-stances were different, we could be friends."

His ear twitched, and he blinked his eyes fast three times in succession. These were different tells I hadn't seen be-fore. What was his game?

"Not sure things would work out too well between the two of us," I said.

"Perhaps. However, that doesn't change the fact that you and I are cut from the same block. That's why I'm willing to strike a deal."

"I haven't heard too many good things about your deals. Never end well."

My chest started to throb. Dull at first, like a burr caught my shirt and rubbing the wrong way. Yet, it didn't take long before the pain increased, and it got hard to breathe. I winced, placing my hand on my side. It came away bloody.

"See, you ain't got long. You're going to pass soon and from the looks of it, you're coming with me."

"What about our arrangement?"

"Let me get to that."

"Sam, no altering the deal, just play the game," Pete said, balling his hand into a fist.

"This doesn't concern you, old man. This is between Jack and me. He started this carousel a spinnin'. Besides, you've lost already, you've folded, so shut your yap."

The old timer frowned but stayed quiet. I tried to study Sam's face for something familiar, anything that would give me an edge as to what he was playing at, but each time I tried, the pain would lance through my body causing a coughing fit.

"Let's forget this game, call it a draw. I'll give you another ten years, and let me tell you, son, they'll be the best years you'll ever have. You want money? Done. You want women? Done. You'll live a life of luxury."

"What's the catch?" I asked, wiping the blood from my mouth with a dirty handkerchief.

"Do I have to spell it out for you? You come live with me when it's over, Jack."

His fingers drummed so loud on the table it hurt my ears. I glanced at my cards again. Aces and Eights, King high. The options weighed on me. On one hand, I could live out a few more years and then be damned to hell. On the other, if my intuition was right, I could win this game and walk away free.

"I don't think so. Show me what you got," I said, laying my cards out on the table.

The smile disappeared from Sam's face, replaced with a sneer. The drumming stopped and he balled his hand into a fist, ripping up pieces of the table with his nails.

Sam flipped his cards over, he had a ten, Jack, Queen, and King. He held onto his last card for a moment before revealing it. It was another Jack.

I smiled and clapped my hands together which brought about another wave of pain. I coughed up a wad of bloody phlegm onto the table and almost fell out of my chair; however, I was able to choke out a couple words.

"I win."

"No, Jack. You lose," Pete said.

"I tried to help, but you wanted to play your game. Cheaters never prosper, Jack." Sam said.

My vision blurred to the point that Sam and Pete were nothing but fuzzy shapes, yet somehow Sam's rictus grin was still clear.

"We had a deal," I said, though my voice came through as a raspy whisper.

"Indeed we did, and we'll honor your deal," Pete said. "We won't be taking you anywhere, and we'll let you be."

I forced a smile onto my face, and even that small act brought about a spasm of pain in my guts. Mustering all the determination I could, I sat back into my chair.

"Fix me up," I said.

Sam made a tsk-tsk sound and shook his head.

"I'm afraid not. Gonna let you be."

My heart dropped into my stomach. "But the deal!"

"Deal was we wouldn't take you anywhere. Nothing in there about making you whole again. Wording, Jack, it's all about the wording," Sam said.

"Sorry, Jack. But you brought this upon yourself. I'm afraid I can't intervene. Goodbye." With those words, Pete disappeared.

"I may be a lot of things, but I follow rules and agreements. So long," Sam said.

The sound of the saloon returned with Sam's disappearance. It happened so quick that it took me off guard for a moment, sending me spinning. However, the sounds were muffled, as if I were at one end of a tunnel and everyone else was at the other.

The pain in my chest was muffled as well, dull. It was still there, but only annoying instead of debilitating.

Somehow, I'd fallen onto the floor. I didn't remember dropping, just one minute I was sitting at the table and the next I was on the ground staring at a pool of blood that must have been mine. People were rushing toward me, but I couldn't hear anything anymore other than the sound of my own breathing, which was getting shorter and shallower by the second.

Things went dark again and for a horrible second. I thought I'd gone blind. I felt around, hoping to feel the dust-covered floorboards, but there was nothing but cool air. At least there was that. Things had gotten so damned hot as of late.

When my eyesight returned, I was back to sitting at the table. There was a mass of folks right next to me crowding around something. I scooted out of the chair to give them some space which is when I noticed what they were crowding around.

My dead body was on the ground. The people weren't crowding around me to help neither. They were picking me clean, grabbing my gun, boots, and my nice pocket watch that was a gift from my pa.

"Bunch of vultures, aren't they, Jack?" Sam said from behind me.

"What the hell?"

"Indeed."

"I'm dead!" I think I wanted to say it as a question, but it came out of my mouth as a statement as I watched the mob take everything of value of my corpse.

"Yes, you are, which brings me to why I'm here," Sam said.

He walked over to my side and looked at my body. He made a tsking sound and then turned to me.

"You came back to drag me to hell?"

"I wish it were that simple, but we had a deal you see. I can't take you, and neither can Heaven it seems, not that they'd want you."

"Then what what's going to happen to me?"

The saloon vanished under a blanket of darkness so thick I didn't think I would even be able to move through it. I'd seen darkness before, spending my fair share of starless nights out in the wilds, but this was something else in entirely.

"Seems like you're going to spend the rest of your existence in Purgatory, Jack. Not a fun place."

The darkness wasn't quiet. Things moved all around me, getting closer every second. Worse than that, the things spoke. I tried to cover my ears, but it only made them speak louder. The voices of dead friends and relatives. My grandpappy telling me that I was a worthless runt that should have died years ago. My mother screaming in agony as my pa buried an ax in her spine. Other *things* spoke as well. Ancient things that wanted to be free from the darkness as much as I did.

There was as snap of fingers followed by a brilliant flash of orange light. It soon dimmed, casting just enough light I could see the ground below my feet. It was covered in wet, decaying leaves that tended to move every so often, as if something were just beneath the surface.

The light came from a piece of coal smoldering in Sam's hand. He no longer smiled at me but instead wore a slight frown. Sam let out a sigh and tossed me the piece of coal. I reached out instinctively and caught it. I almost dropped it to the ground, halfway expecting it to burn me, but it didn't. Not at first anyway. The longer I held onto it, the warmer it got. It didn't take long before I had to transfer it from hand to hand.

"No, Jack. You see, I really do like you. It takes guts to hustle the devil. That's why I'm leaving you with that gift. Don't lose it, because I don't think you want to be out here in the dark all lonesome and such."

With that, he was gone.

I bounced the burning coal in my hand as I walked. I walked for hours with nothing but the maddening noises of the dark to keep me company. I tried to use my coat to carry the stone, but it muffled the soft light and the *things* got too close for comfort.

As I continued along, I came to a pumpkin patch which was the first different thing I'd seen since arriving. With nothing else to do, I pulled out my knife and started carving one of the pumpkins. It would make an excellent lantern in which to carry the glowing coal. Something to light my way.

"Follow Me"

Theresa sat against a large pine as she finished her beer. She'd been sitting there for three hours, and other than an angry squirrel that occasionally screamed at her, she hadn't seen a thing. No bucks, not even a doe she could maybe *pretend* was a buck.

Her husband, Dale, had done this more than once, heading home in the dark and butchering the animal in the garage. Meat was meat, right? And if you didn't get caught, it didn't happen. Theresa hoped that Dale had better luck, as he would sometimes get into one of his *moods* if he didn't get a deer.

Theresa grabbed another beer from her pack and cracked it open. The pop of the top made her cringe, and for a moment, she considered perhaps being quieter would help in her hunting efforts. Mule deer were skittish by nature. Then again, what was a hunting trip without a beer (or six)? Hell, if she wanted to just shoot a deer, she could have went down to the Miller's farm at the end of the road instead of driving for six hours to the top of the mountain.

Hell, she could have done a lot more at the Miller's too, while Dale was away. It wouldn't be the first time.

Theresa took a swig and grimaced. The beer was warm. However, she was a professional and could outdrink most guys she met. She shifted on the ground and gritted her teeth, as her butt had gone numb. Little pinpricks of feeling started to flood through her behind, but it was part of the experience. At least, that was what Dale had told her.

She looked at her watch. If she didn't see anything soon, she'd head back to the road and meet up with Dale. Theresa was about to pack up her things when a twig snapped nearby. Her heart skipped a beat as she scanned the area. It was just more of the same, pines and aspens. However, she knew from experience that deer could blend in with their surroundings easily.

She made a slow grab for her rifle. It was a hand-me-down from Dale, an old .30-.30. Theresa didn't mind, and she was a good shot on the worst of days. Better than Dale even, although he would never admit it. He always had some lame-ass excuse to protect his manhood: it was too windy; maybe the sight had gotten knocked around in the truck; some dirt flew in his eye... anything other than just admitting she was better at something than he was. It was why she secretly hoped to get something to show him she could do it.

Theresa looked through the trees, trying to find the source of the noise. She slowed her breathing as best she could and listened.

There was another snap, this time accompanied by the woody thunk of antler hitting a low-hanging branch. Her heart began to beat faster with anticipation.

She raised the rifle and watched. Soon, it came closer. Theresa caught a glimpse of the huge rack of antlers as they pushed through the brush. This was a monster!

She placed her finger on the trigger, and as she did, a thousand thoughts raced through her mind. Would it give her a broadside shot? What would Dale think if she shot a monster buck and he didn't get anything? Would he be happy? Or would he get jealous? Theresa didn't like the jealous Dale. Jealous Dale would sometimes get handsy in a bad way.

Those thoughts washed away as the buck stepped into the open.

It was beautiful.

The buck was larger than any muley she'd seen before. It was a thick four-point with two drop tines. It was the kind of trophy most only dreamed about. She tried not to think about it too hard and focus on her shot.

Theresa aimed right behind the shoulder, just like she had practiced hundreds of times. She exhaled, then held her breathe. Just another second and it would be done.

The buck looked up and then bounded away before she could squeeze the trigger.

Theresa watched it bound away and disappear up the mountainside. She looked around dumbfounded and tried to figure out what had just happened. A moment later, Dale stepped out into the clearing on the opposite side of the deer.

He'd spooked it.

For half a second, she thought about sending a round his way. It was a fleeting thought, but one that made her smile on the inside, nonetheless.

"Dammit! I almost had it, and you scared it away!"

The words came out of her mouth coated with poison and she winced. That kind of tone usually didn't end well for her. However, this was a unique situation.

Dale stood by the tall pines with a blank expression. If he was concerned about what had just happened or even the way she had snapped at him, it didn't show. Instead, Dale waved her over. "Follow me."

"What? Did you get one?"

He waved again and then stepped back into the trees.

Theresa cursed. Her legs and butt groaned as she stretched, but Dale was already out of sight. The bastard wasn't even going to wait for her. She growled, grabbed her things, and chugged the rest of her lukewarm beer. Then, she threw the can into the pile of empties on the forest floor and hurried after him.

The timber was thick, and the sun was starting to set, making it difficult to see. Theresa thought about grabbing her headlamp out of her pack, but she didn't want to stop and fish around for it. Dale was nothing more than a silhouette in the distance, and he'd get awful cranky if she didn't listen.

"Hey!" Theresa shouted, hoping he would stop.

She jogged forward, taking care to not trip on a rock or fallen branch. Ahead in the distance, Dale stopped and waved her over again.

"Follow me."

Theresa stopped. His voice was quiet, almost a whisper. It was as if he had said those words standing right next to her, though he was more than a hundred yards away. Dale turned and began trekking through the woods again. She didn't like this at all, but she didn't want to lose sight of him again as it was only getting darker.

Theresa ran after him. "Wait up!"

If Dale heard (which she figured he did), he ignored her and kept moving. What the hell was his problem? If he would just wait a couple of seconds, she could catch up and they could go together to wherever the hell he was leading.

Theresa did her best to keep up; however, he was always just a few steps too far ahead. The sun fell behind the tall mountain peaks. As it left, so too did the warmth. Theresa's anger kept her going. She didn't like getting led through the trees like a dog. If Dale had something he wanted to show her, he could at least wait. This was nothing short of bullshit.

The forest grew thicker and darker as they went. There were many times Theresa had to put her arms in front of her face and push through branches. Dale stayed ahead of her regardless of how fast she moved.

"Dammit, wait for me!"

The trees got thicker, and in the dusk, almost appeared larger or... older. The thought crossed her mind, and she wasn't too sure where it had come from. Of course, it was the same forest she had spent most the day in, but it felt different. Theresa couldn't pinpoint the exact details of it all, but deep down... no! Theresa shook her head to clear her mind. It was just her brain playing tricks, or maybe the beers had gotten to her.

Dale crashed through the brush ahead of her and then the forest went silent. It happened so fast that Theresa stopped. She stared ahead through the trees trying to catch sight of Dale, but it was thick with shadows and darkness.

"Dale?"

"Follow me."

She jumped, and his words sent chills up her spine. Theresa double checked to make sure there was still a round in the chamber of her rifle. Who knew what was out here? Bears, cougars... Hell, maybe she could still fill her tag if a buck decided to step out in front of her. They were far enough back that even if she shot, it would be hard for anyone to pinpoint their location. It was a risk, but if that monster buck stepped out again, it was a risk she was willing to take.

Theresa listened for Dale—for anything. There was nothing but the sound of her own breathing.

Theresa tightened her grip on the gun and stepped through the trees.

Dale stood in a small clearing with his back towards her. There was something at his feet, but Theresa couldn't quite tell what it was. With a wave of his hand, he motioned her closer.

"Follow me."

It was the same monotone voice he'd been using since he first showed up. Something was up. Theresa felt it in her marrow, but she couldn't quite figure out what. Had he shot another doe? If so, he didn't have to be so mysterious about it. Just fess up and she'd help him gut it and load it up in the truck (discreetly of course). They had seen a fish and game cop the first day they came up here, but that was it.

"What's that there?" she asked, pointed the rifle to the pile at Dale's feet.

"Follow me."

She took a couple of shaky steps forward, and Dale turned towards her. His eyes caught the last bit of light in the sky, and for half a second, they lit up like a cat's eyes in the dark. Theresa stopped and stared at him, but his eyes were normal. It happened so fast that Theresa figured it was her mind playing tricks. Dale stepped over whatever was on the ground and pointed at the pile.

It was too dark to see what the pile was. She took another step and dozens of fireflies lit up just in front her. She and found herself standing just outside a ring of white and red mushrooms that ran in a circle around Dale and the thing at his feet. The fireflies were beautiful, but at the same time, it was too weird. To her knowledge, there weren't any fireflies up in these mountains.

Theresa gave the mushrooms a closer look. Mushrooms in the mountains weren't uncommon, especially after a heavy rain. She had kept her eye out for some of those magic mushrooms everyone talked about, but in reality, she had no clue what she was looking for and didn't want to eat the wrong kind. The wrong kind would leave her dead in a pile of her own feces. However, as common as mushrooms were, she had never in her life seen mushrooms like these, nor in a circle like this.

"What in the hell?"

Instead of answering, Dale pointed to the ground again.

Theresa shuffled closer and looked at what he was pointing at. She expected to see a dead deer or something. Or hell, maybe even an elk that Dale had gotten too antsy with. What she didn't expect, was Dale's bloody body. He had a horrified look etched into his face, forever frozen in death. He had died screaming.

Theresa let out a shout and stumbled back.

"What in the hell? What... Dale?!"

She looked up, and the other Dale's eyes flashed with an azure glow. A dozen more eyes lit up behind him. He smiled at her, and even through the dimly lit forest, his many rows of sharp teeth were visible.

She tried to raise her rifle, but dozens of small hands grabbed her from behind, tearing through clothes and flesh with ease. The things dragged her to the ground with their combined weight. All the while, the thing that had been Dale stared at her with a vicious smile. He grew taller and taller until he towered over her.

Mighty antlers crowned the thing's head, and it gave her a wet chuckle.

Theresa's screams echoed through the forest.

"The Angler"

I've been around for quite some time now. Some like to crack jokes and say I'm older than dirt. I guess in a sense, it's true. I don't even know how old I am anymore, not that it matters really. Needless to say, I've seen some things. I mean, if I were to start listing all my experiences, you'd probably move along not believing a dang thing I said. I wouldn't blame you. I hardly believe it either, but it's all true. But those stories are for another time. This story is about how I like fishing. It's one of my favorite pastimes, actually.

There's just something about sitting there, waiting for something to come near and get hooked. It doesn't matter how many times I catch something; it always fills me with a bit of excitement. I guess you could say it's really one of the only forms of delight I partake in these days. Well, outside of actually eating my catch that is.

It's not even just about catching my prey and eating them. You could say it's a moral duty! You see, sometimes fish can get overpopulated, and when that happens, they begin to destroy the ecosystem. These days, I focus on culling that overpopulation. I feel like I'm doing my part to keep this world in balance.

You know, there are even creatures deep in the sea called anglerfish that can lure prey close by lighting up a tiny little appendage on their head called a luminescent fin ray. It acts as a lure in the dark, and other fish will swim close and then the anglerfish will devour them whole. Fascinating creatures.

I'm kind of the same. In my many years upon this land, I've found patience is quite the virtue, and the best things come to those who wait.

Sometimes all it takes is a little light in the darkness to catch the curious.

Jack turned up the radio and hit the high beams. It was dark out, and the high canyon walls made it even darker. Sleep pulled at his eyes, trying its best to get him to take a little snooze, but the loud music and worry of a deer darting out in front of him were enough to keep him somewhat alert. His brother, Tanner, had a hit a deer in this very canyon just two years ago. He said it appeared out of thin air. One moment he was bebopping down the road a nd—

BAM!

—he tore into the critter going just a little over sixty. The impact obliterated the deer. Unfortunately, the deer also destroyed his truck, which was too bad. It had been a nice truck. Now Tanner had to drive a beat-up old Bronco that was on its last leg, and he couldn't turn his neck all the way to right anymore without wincing.

Jack let out a big yawn. As he did, his tires brushed across the rumble strips near the shoulder, causing the entire truck to vibrate. He brought his vehicle back to the center of the lane and shook his head.

This was ridiculous. Jack knew he should have pulled over and caught some ZZZs at that last rest stop before entering the canyon, but home was only an hour away. He could make it an hour, right?

Jack reached down into a small cooler and pulled out an ice-cold energy drink. He hadn't wanted to drink it this late, as he'd be up for hours when he finally got home, but in the end, he decided it was better to be awake all night than dead on the side of the road.

The cold liquid tickled his throat as he drank it and some of the carbonation went up into his sinus cavity. Jack grunted and then rubbed his forehead and squinted until the feeling disappeared. When he opened his eyes, he found a mule deer standing in the road.

It lolled its head to the side to stare at him as the truck bore down upon the animal.

Jack hit the brakes, and his truck skidded on the asphalt. His headlights lit up the deer's eyes. Instead of being wide-eyed, the animal appeared sluggish, almost sleepy. That thought stuck with him despite everything that was happening.

Fate was on Jack's side, and he stopped the truck less than a foot away from the animal. Jack and the deer stared at one another for what felt like minutes. Then, the deer limped away.

Jack watched it go. Its hindquarters were matted with blood, and it dragged one leg behind it as if it was nothing but meat and mush.

He got out of his truck just as the animal disappeared into the nearby pines, eaten by the shadows. It made a strange bleating mew that sounded like a pained warning bark. A few more branches snapped, and then it was gone.

Jack inspected the front of his truck to see if perhaps he'd hit the animal and didn't know it. He expected to see something on the grill given how messed up that deer was, but there was no damage to his vehicle. There wasn't even a bit of fur nor a speck of blood.

"What in the heck is going on?" Jack looked around, but he couldn't find anything that would have caused that kind of a wound on that deer. He did, however, find bloody tracks leading up the road.

Jack moved his truck over to the shoulder and grabbed his coat as well as a small flashlight he always kept in his glove compartment. Then, he followed the tracks.

They led up the road a ways. It was quiet out, so quiet even the bugs weren't making a ruckus. The only sound was the crunch of his boots in the soft gravel on the side of the road and his breathing. His heavy breathing.

Jack vowed to hit the gym more, starting next week for sure. Maybe he would even lay off the junk food a bit. The road curved sharply up ahead. The locals called it a Deadman's curve, as sleepy and drunken drivers would often lose their lives at that very spot. Given the crumpled state of the guardrail, Jack surmised the turn had claimed another poor soul not too long ago.

He lost sight of his truck as he followed the curve, but as he cleared the mountainside, his heart quickened. Up ahead was an old sedan with its hazard lights on. The driver's side door was open, as well as the interior dome light.

Jack stopped. He had the unpleasant sensation that something was watching him—waiting for him. Something hungry.

A part of him wanted to run back to the truck and just keep on moving until he was back home. Yet a small part of him, a part saturated with the silky sweetness of curiosity, pulled him forward.

"Hello?"

Nobody answered. He shined the flashlight around, and the beam cut through the dark like a knife, but it did little to dispel the gloom surrounding the car up ahead.

Jack pulled out his cell phone, but he was effectively in a dead zone, as there weren't any bars. There was only a small patch in the canyon that didn't have any service. Of course, the car had to be stuck in the dead zone.

Perhaps the owner had wandered off up ahead to try and get some bars and make a call. Or maybe they were hurt. His mind flashed back to Tanner hitting that deer a couple years ago. Jack needed to see if the owner was okay.

He quickened his pace as he sauntered up to the car. It appeared to be an early 90s Plymouth that once had been blue or maybe purple. Weather had taken its toll on the vehicle, and now it was just a light shade of sun-blasted indigo.

The vanity plate read ANG13R. A worn bumper sticker that said *Gone Fishing* was starting to peel up. Jack figured the sticker was probably just as old as the car itself.

The rhythmic chime of the door-open warning filled his ears as it warbled through the crisp mountain air. Jack's face scrunched in confusion. It was like the noise started just as he had gotten close to the car. He figured he should have heard that before he'd seen the sedan.

It didn't matter. Maybe it was just old and had a short.

Jack shined his flashlight through the car's windows. They were covered with dust and some sort of greasy grime. The backseat was plastered in what looked like blood and bits of brown hair.

The deer's bloody tracks lead from the rear driver's side door down the road. Jack circled the car and found the front of the vehicle had a large dent in the bumper and part of the hood had crumpled. He leaned in close and found more blood and hair.

Part of the mystery was starting to come together. Jack figured the driver probably hit the deer and decided to take it home for whatever reason. Maybe the driver saw it as free meat. Or maybe driver got in the car, headed down the road as the deer bled all over the backseat, and then the animal woke up. Not dead at all. It probably started thrashing around, causing the driver the pull over and get out.

The story made sense in Jack's mind. Except, where was the driver now?

Jack cupped his hands and yelled as loud as he could. "Hey? Are you okay? Do you need any help?"

Nobody answered. Jack circled the car again. He stopped at the driver's side door and peered in. The interior was hot and muggy, like the inside of a greenhouse. A stink like sour milk and rotten meat crawled up his nose. It made him want to throw up his energy drink, but he fought the feeling into submission. Jack figured it was probably bits of the mangled deer. Who in their right mind would put a bloody carcass in the back of their car? Then again, it wasn't like the car was in pristine condition to begin with.

Jack leaned in through the door and peered into the back seat. It was a crime scene. There was a lot more blood than Jack had seen before.

He didn't like it. Something didn't add up, and he needed to get out of there. As he backed out of the car, the glove box popped open.

Jack screamed and reared back, hitting the back of his head on the ceiling of the car. He let out of grunt of pain and massaged his skull. A bit of his hair stuck to the roof of the car as if it were covered in some sort of glue. Jack didn't even want to think what it actually was. He just pulled his head away until his hair detached from the car and slapped against his scalp.

"Son of a..."

As he rubbed his throbbing head, something in the glove box caught his eye. It was a wallet.

Perhaps it had the driver's information in it and would let him know who to send the search party for. Jack reached for the wallet but stopped as he got closer to the glove box. A white chunk of something appeared to attach the wallet to the inside of the compartment, like a tendon or ligament. The stringy substance pulsed, and Jack swore the car shuddered when it did.

The hairs on the back of his neck stood up straight, and his flesh broke out in goosebumps. It was time to go.

Jack tried to back out of the car, but his foot caught in the driver's side seatbelt. He struggled to break free, but the more he kicked, the more tangled his foot got. He tried to turn onto his back so he'd have both hands free to work on the seatbelt, but his hand became wedged between the seat and the center console. When he pulled his hand out, something latched into his skin. Pain flared across his hand and up his arm.

He screamed and yanked back, finally freeing his hand. However, his hand came back with only nine fingers. His pinky was just a bloody stump.

Jack yelled and clutched his wounded hand to his chest as blood sprayed across the interior of the Plymouth.

The dome light flicked off, and he swore he heard the rumble of the engine starting, only it didn't sound like a motor. It sounded more like a guttural growl.

As Jack went to sit up, something sharp dug into his back and held him place. Jack cried for help. Nobody could hear his screams.

The interior of the vehicle seemed to close in on him. He struggled with all his might to break free, but it was like a mouse trying to break free from a cat's maw.

Jack's screams echoed through the canyon.

Before the sun came up, an early 90s Plymouth that once had been blue or maybe purple glided down the road. The grime-covered windows made it impossible to see the driver, but the dent in the grill made it appear as if the car were smiling.

"Degrading"

Ryker let out a sigh of relief as he walked into the lab. Corporate kept the climate chilled to maintain subject and equipment integrity, and it was a nice contrast to the surface where temps reached 120 degrees or more. Hell, Ryker considered anything under 100 a cold front.

The novelty of the temperature wore off after an hour. After three hours, he couldn't stop shivering without wearing his worn-out parka that maybe used to be green.

He checked the clock. It had been almost nine hours since he started his shift.

Machines and computers buzzed in the background. He had several programs up and running, but the most important, other than the subject himself, was the signal strength monitor. Ryker glanced over to the bright ruby glow of the numbers.

92%

It had dropped two percent in the last hour. Ryker made a note in the logbook. He dreaded the mountain of paperwork that would come his way if it reached 90% during his watch.

The universe had a sick sense of humor. The signal dropped to 91%.

"Come on... Just hold steady for another hour."

It dropped again.

And again.

Then a large warning banner appeared on his screen.

CONTACT WEAK

Shitball sandwiches! Contact with the subject was vital to the mission! Without contact, well, Ryker didn't want to think of the consequences. He knew trying to maintain signal strength would be next to impossible as the tether between the subject and the package would rapidly begin to degrade.

The signal dropped from 90% to 89%, and alarms blared to life, filling the small lab with deafening klaxons.

Ryker stood, sending his folding chair flying to the ground. "No, no, no, no, no!"

He opened a different program and started typing, his fingers a blur. A deep voice crackled on the intercom.

Status?

"I'm looking into it."

The signal strength continued to fall.

75%

Ryker looked over his monitor to the back of the lab. A clearsteel tube sat suspended in the air. The indicator lights on the tube flashed and filled the room with a mix of blues and reds. Something thumped against the walls from inside the tube.

Franklin stumbled out of bed and to the bathroom. He turned on the lights and they flickered to life, causing the room to spin. Franklin grabbed onto the side of the sink to steady himself. It wouldn't do to fall, hit his head on the side of the tub, and die naked on the floor of the bathroom. He could see the headlines now. *Middle-Aged Nobody Found Dead in a Puddle of Urine and Vomit.*

He barely made it over the toilet bowl before he threw up. At least he had that much going for him.

Franklin knelt down next to the toilet. The cool ceramic felt nice against his body, but the smells of the water, stale piss, and what he just puked up hit him in the face, and he let loose again.

Franklin glanced at his watch. The digital numbers flashed and got stuck on 75. He tapped the watch a couple of times, and they flashed again, finally telling him it was just past four in the morning.

The numbers. It reminded him of that lab dream he continued to have. Always the same person sitting in the chair. A younger man with a dead eye, fuzzy caterpillar mustache, and that horrible green jacket.

After Franklin felt like he was done calling dinosaurs through the porcelain scrying bowl, he flushed away the foul contents. As the water spun and took away the mess, something slithered through the murky water just before disappearing down the drain.

"What the hell?"

He looked closer, but it was gone now. He chalked it up to still being drunk and his mind playing tricks on him.

Franklin walked over to the sink. He rinsed the rancid taste from his mouth and washed his face. Letters appeared on the mirror as they would on a computer monitor.

CONTACT WEAK

Franklin stopped cleaning his face and leaned closer to the mirror, but the words were gone. Only his ragged face with dark bags under his eyes and deep wrinkles etched into his skin stared back. It was probably time (or past time) he took care of himself. He vowed to hit the gym in the morning, or at least the evening. Or maybe once this week.

Franklin shuffled back to his bed and passed out.

He once again dreamt of that man in the lab. Others had joined him, and they all screamed and pointed at something behind him. Franklin turned to see what it was, but alarms blared to life, alarms that sounded like his cell phone.

He woke to a phone call. Franklin groaned and reached for the phone and accidentally knocked it off the night-stand. It continued to ring, but he flipped it the bird and rolled over. He contemplated trying to go back to sleep when it rang again.

"Okay! Bejesus krispies!"

He leaned over the side of the bed and reached for the phone. As he did, a black tentacle slid out from under the frame and moved towards his hand.

Franklin screamed and snatched his hand back. His heart hammered against his chest. Blood poured from his nose.

"No, fucking way. What was that?"

He watched the floor from the edge of the bed like he was a kid, afraid the boogeyman would get him. His phone's screen turned off and darkness filled the room.

A wet, sucking noise came from under the bed. Franklin's leg started to shake. He reached over to turn on the lamp and bumped it instead. It fell to the floor, and the wet noise got louder.

Something grabbed onto the bedsheet and pulled.

"Fuck me! Help!"

Whatever had a hold on the bedsheets yanked on them. Franklin tried to scream, but the blood from his nose filled his mouth, and it came out as a gurgle. He found himself in a tug-of-war with the thing.

His phone rang again, filling the room with a soft blue glow. As soon as it turned on, the thing stopped tugging and the wet noise disappeared.

Franklin peered over the edge of the bed. His phone lay on the carpet, but there wasn't any sign of the black tentacle. He knew as soon as he reached for it, that *thing* would get him.

The phone continued to ring, but he knew it would soon stop, and then he'd be bathed in darkness again. Franklin took a deep breath. Then, as quickly as humanly possible, he snatched his phone from the floor.

Nothing grabbed him. No slimy tentacles appeared from under there. The ringing stopped, and Franklin turned on the phone's flashlight.

Perhaps the booze was messing with him. Or maybe the lack of sleep. Or it could have been the weed the woman sold him last night. Maybe it was laced with something.

That had to be it. Just a mixture of poor choices.

Franklin grabbed the lamp off the floor and put it back on the nightstand. He turned it on, and it filled the room with a dull yellow glow.

Just to be sure there wasn't some sort of horrifying creature under the bed, he turned on the phone's camera and snapped a pic. The flash went off. For some reason, he expected to hear some sort of inhuman squealing, but nothing like that happened.

He looked at the picture on his phone. The mess under the bed disgusted him, but other than dirty clothes, garbage, and some other items that probably needed to be quarantined or incinerated, there wasn't anything else. Franklin did catch his reflection on the screen though. Blood ran from both nostrils and covered his chin and chest.

"Nice."

As he made his way to the bathroom to take a shower, he checked his voicemail.

It was his boss, Jared.

Franklin, where the fuck are you? You were supposed to be here over an hour ago. If you don't get here ASAP... No, you know what? Don't even worry about it. You're fired!

Ryker watched the signal drop from 70% to 62%. He pointed at the screen.

"See! It keeps dropping. What's going on?" he asked.

Three technicians stood next to him. They each wore a heavy-duty bio-chem protective suit that covered their whole body. They looked at the screen and then to the clearsteel tube in unison. Ryker thought the helmets with the darkened glass visors were a bit much. If they thought the lab was that dangerous, then why didn't he get the same kind of gear?

"This is abnormal," the tech said. The mic in his helmet modulated his voice and it came out tinny.

Ryker threw his hands in the air. "And you went to specialized training for this hypothesis? No shit! How do we stop it? At this rate, the signal strength will drop to zero in less than six hours."

The second tech did some calculations on his datapad. "Actually, at this rate, you'll lose the signal in one hour, twenty-three minutes, and two seconds. Give or take ten seconds."

Ryker wanted to stab a hole into the man's suit with a pen and watch him cry like a baby. But that wouldn't help anything.

"Okay, less than two hours then, thank you. What do we do?"

Something wet slapped the inside of the tube. Condensation made it hard to make out anything but the human-shaped silhouette, but there was also something else. Something that writhed and wriggled.

Ryker took a step back and pointed. "That will hold it, yeah?"

None of the techs answered. Two of them gathered their gear and left. The third started to leave, but Ryker grabbed him by the shoulder. "Hey! That will hold it, right? What do we do?"

The man shrugged away from Ryker's hand as if it were contaminated with the plague. Perhaps it was for all Ryker knew.

The tech stared at him. Or at least Ryker thought he was staring at him. It was hard to tell through the visor.

"You want my advice?"

Ryker held his hands out wide. "Yeah, that's what you're supposed to do."

"Try and message the subject. Speed things up. Help him achieve his objective before you lose the signal or... Well, you know what happens."

"Message him? That's against protocol."

The tech shrugged and left. The door closed behind the man. Ryker still had more questions, so he went to follow him, but the door wouldn't open.

Ryker growled and tried to use his badge. A red light flashed.

Access denied.

Ryker tried again and got the same results.

He stumbled back and sat in his chair. Those bastards had locked him in. He hit the intercom button.

"What the hell?! Let me out of here!"

The deep voice of the intercom crackled to life.

Unless the objective is successfully completed, you may not leave the laboratory. You know the protocol.

"Come on! This isn't fair! You let me out of here!"

The intercom's static died. Ryker growled and spun around. More wet slaps and thuds came from the tube. The signal had dropped to 59%.

Protocol be damned; he was going to message the subject.

When Franklin got out of the shower, he found a new text message on his phone. The clock on the screen read 59. Franklin tapped the phone and it fixed itself, just like his watch had. Whatever drugs he'd consumed last night, they apparently were still messing with him.

The text came from an unknown number. It read:

Get to work. You're running out of time! You know what you're supposed to do.

Had Jared changed his mind? Why didn't he just call? Maybe the message had been a show for the other employees to scare them or something. As much as he hated to admit it, Franklin needed the job. His rent was due in a week, and his cupboards were almost empty.

Franklin brushed his teeth. Once he finished, he rinsed his mouth out with water and then spit. He expected to see bits of food or other crap, but what he didn't expect to see was so much blood and a tooth.

He felt around in his mouth and found the empty spot where the tooth had come out. Some of his others were loose as well. Franklin wiggled one out of morbid curiosity, but as he did, something touched his finger.

Something slimy.

Something that moved on its own.

Franklin pulled his hand away. He opened his mouth wide and looked in the mirror. Other than irritated gums and a missing tooth, nothing looked out of the ordinary.

He was going crazy; he knew it. Franklin wanted to call 911 and go to the hospital. However, he couldn't afford a trip to the ER, and he needed to get his ass to work to save his job before it was too late.

Franklin got dressed and hopped in the car. Luckily, traffic was in his favor, and he arrived at JJJ's Cleaning Service in record time. The windowless building acted as more of a storage facility where Jared kept all the cleaning supplies and his tiny fleet of vans that shouldn't have been street-legal due to disrepair.

Franklin walked through the front door, and the harsh smell of cleaning chemicals hit his nose and stung his eyes. As he walked down the hall towards Jared's office, his stomach twisted. The hallway started to spin, and he had to lean against the wall to steady himself.

He veered from Jared's office into the restroom just in time to puke into the sink. The vomit was a mix of blood and bile, and... what in the shit were those? Thousands of pale translucent worms wriggled through the vomit like it was a swimming pool.

Franklin stared at the sink in horror.

The toilet flushed, and Franklin whipped around. Jared's bald head peeked above the stall door.

Franklin quickly turned on the water to the sink and washed whatever he had thrown up down the drain. The worms writhed as the water swept them away.

"Well, look who it is," Jared said as he stepped out of the stall. He zipped his pants up and walked over, stopping about two feet away to throw a hand over his nose. "What in the name of God did you eat?"

Franklin's stomach gurgled in response, and he fought the urge to spew right into Jared's dumb-fuck face.

"You know what? It doesn't matter. I don't even want to know what kind of debased things you're into. It's a good thing you're here; you can clean out your locker."

Jared pushed past Franklin without even washing his hands. Franklin followed him out into the hallway. "Look, I'm sorry. I haven't been feeling well."

Jared sighed and rolled his eyes. "You haven't been feeling well for over two months now. Enough is enough. Get your shit and leave."

He started to walk away, but Franklin pushed past him and stood in his way. "Look, I need this job, okay? I'll work every weekend this month, and you won't have to log it as overtime."

Jared looked at the floor and scratched his head. "Fine. Your little boy-toy called in sick today. So if you want to keep your job, you go work his location."

Franklin's stomach roiled again, and his legs began to shake. What he needed was to go back home and sleep, but he couldn't let this opportunity to keep his job slip away.

"Okay, I'm on it."

Jared smiled. "Good. It's that house up on Hangar Hill."

Franklin's heart dropped to his knees. It had to be that place, didn't it?

"Is there a problem?" Jared asked. The look in his eye told Franklin that Jared knew about the house on Hangar Hill.

"No. No problem at all."

"Good, then get going." Jared's face morphed into the man in Franklin's dreams. "Do your job and finish the objective."

Ryker watched the signal strength drop to 50%. But then miraculously it stopped there. He checked the equipment. All the indicators showed green, and the program ran steady. Hell, even the thumper in the clearsteel tube stopped thrashing.

Hopefully, everything was back on track. Just finish the objective, and we can all go home tonight.

Ryker was sure that if he made it out of this he would get punished for breaking protocol. They weren't supposed to send messages once an operative was in place. It was too dangerous. The big heads back in Research and Development had mentioned something about playing with quantum entanglement or something like that. Ryker didn't understand a word of their gibberish, and chalked it up to the smartasses fucking with the regular folk.

Just finish the objective, please.

Blood ran from Ryker's nose, spilling onto the desk.

Franklin drove out of the city towards Hangar Hill. There used to be an old military airfield there during World War II. After the war, the military shut the field down. Back in the '50s the Davidson family bought the property, built a mansion on it, and refurbished the airstrip for their private use.

The family still owned the estate, but nobody lived there anymore. However, JJJ Cleaning somehow got a contract to clean the place once a month. It didn't make sense to Franklin, but hey, money was money, and a job was a job. However, nobody liked cleaning that house. It felt... *off*.

Electrical equipment never worked right. There wasn't any cell service up there. The house could have easily been the centerpiece of a ghost movie.

Franklin had been lucky enough to avoid Hangar Hill during his time at JJJ. However, as he drove the switchbacks up the hill, and the mansion came into view, he had the strongest case of déjà vu.

A chain-link fence surrounded the property. The fence once had privacy slats; however, many of them had broken and disappeared over the years. Street lights lined either side of the road, but like the fence, most of them were broken. Franklin wanted to be done with everything and out of there before the sun went down anyway.

The road led to a rusty, steel gate that blocked the entrance. It sported a length of chain and an industrial-strength padlock.

Franklin put the van in park and stepped out. The cool air washed across his skin. Franklin mentally kicked himself in the ass for forgetting his hoodie. Hopefully, it wasn't as chilly inside the house.

He pulled the keys from his belt and looked for one that matched the padlock. Finally, he found the one that fit and turned the key. The padlock clicked open. At the same time, a slight tremor shook beneath his feet, and the hair on the back of his neck stood. His skin broke out in a cold sweat, and he started coughing.

Franklin couldn't stop coughing, each one wracking his chest harder than the last. He put his hand up against his mouth and it came away slick with blood and spittle. What in the hell was happening?

Franklin wanted to drive back home, leave Hangar Hill in the rearview, and crawl under the covers for a few days. He still felt ill from his bender last night.

His phone buzzed with a text. Franklin shuffled back to the van and climbed in before pulling the phone out of his pocket. Back in the van, his coughing subsided. He took a few deep breaths and then checked the text.

Finish your objective quickly!

Franklin texted back and then drove up to the mansion.

Ryker's screen blipped with an incoming message. He froze, unsure of what to do. He never in a million years thought that he would get a response.

Ryker clicked on the message icon and opened it.

#4@fct#53t 3tdged... *fu#k! I'll get it #@DT*

Ryker checked the signal. It hadn't dropped at all in the last ten minutes. Maybe, just maybe, they could do this. The world couldn't afford any more dimensional borers.

Franklin stepped out of the van and grabbed his keys and his cleaning supplies. The mansion stood three stories tall, and he knew from the others that it had a basement—and possibly even a sub-basement, although nobody had been able to get the door open.

His job involved vacuuming all the accessible floors, dusting the uncovered surfaces, and ensuring everything was still in working order. By all accounts, it was a simple job. But Hangar Hill loomed oppressively over everyone who stepped foot on the property.

The heavy oak front door to the mansion stood over ten feet tall. A huge metal knocker shaped like a horned beast with three eyes adorned the burgundy-stained wood.

It gave Franklin the willies, and he couldn't bring himself to look it in the eyes, afraid that they would blink.

Franklin easily found the key to the front door on his key ring. He didn't even need to read the label, as it was bigger than the others, black. Whoever had made the key etched a symbol into the metal that was shaped like two triangles next to one another.

Franklin unlocked the door and swung it open. Motes of dust swirled in the sunlight. The room led to a grand greeting room with a piano covered in a white sheet, some couches similarly covered, and twin staircases leading up to the next level.

This was as good of a place to start as any, so Franklin shut the door behind him and got to work. It was going to be a long day, and he already felt like a day-old dog turd.

Franklin started with the vacuum. He was only halfway through the entry when the power flickered and died, shrouding him in darkness.

"Fuck me!"

He fished out his phone and turned on the flashlight. The darkness of the house closed in, suffocating him. Something flopped on the floor behind the stairs. It happened suddenly, and Franklin froze.

Then it flopped again, and Franklin could only imagine a wet fish writhing on the floor. His heart threatened to pound out of his chest.

The thing moved closer.

Franklin shined his light in that direction, but there wasn't anything there. He walked backward toward the door, keeping his light on the stairs as he reached behind him with one hand, feeling for the doorknob.

He touched the wood of the door and searched, frantic to find the knob. From beneath his feet, in the basement, something heavy thudded against the floor.

Franklin screamed, spun around, and opened the door. Sunlight washed the shadows away. He ran outside and called Jared.

"JJJ's Cleaning. How can I help you?"

"Hey, it's Franklin."

Jared sighed. "What is it now?"

"The power's out in the house and I thi—"

"Look. I'm tired of your shit. Finish your job, or you're fired for real."

"But the—"

"But nothing! The breakers are in the basement. Finish it, or you can forget about your paycheck too."

Jared ended the call. Franklin stood outside the mansion, his heart still racing. Part of him wanted to say screw it and leave. He felt like shit, apparently had to deal with hallucinations now, and the house gave him the creeps. Besides, he was pretty sure that Jared couldn't withhold his paycheck for work he'd already done.

However, the other part of him argued that he was acting foolishly. Just go down there, flip the breakers, and get back to work. An hour—two, tops—and he'd be done and could go back home.

He grabbed the flashlight from the van's glove compartment and headed back into the house. The flashlight cast a bigger and brighter beam, plus now he didn't have to drain his phone's battery. Once inside, Franklin shined the light over by the stairs but didn't see anything out of the ordinary. It had to have been his imagination.

Having never been inside the house, he had no idea how to get to the basement. Franklin eventually found himself in a kitchen that was bigger than some of the restaurants he had worked in. Hell, he could have fit his old apartment inside the space. The faint *plink-plink-plink* of a leaky faucet echoed through the room.

The lack of windows made the room pitch black, but the flashlight did its job and cut a path through the gloom. A door stood at the other end of the kitchen, and Franklin hoped it would lead him to the basement.

As he walked past the sink, something thumped from inside it. Water splashed up and out the sides and sprinkled his arm and cheeks, stopping him in his tracks.

Franklin froze. He told himself it was only his imagination, just like the other times. Yet, the splashing continued, and whatever wallowed in the sink slapped the sides and made a low, gurgling mewl.

He closed his eyes, took a deep breath, and counted backward from ten in his head. As he did, the thing started thrashing violently and squealing louder. However, when he got to one, it stopped.

His nose started to bleed again, and he wiped it away with a handkerchief from his back pocket.

Franklin decided against looking in the sink. He didn't want to see what was in there and found the idea of finding nothing in there equally frightening. He walked over to the door and opened it.

Bingo!

A long set of stairs led down to the basement. They creaked and groaned as he walked down. The air grew cooler as well. Not just regular basement cool—this chill had to be manmade, like an air conditioner. The stairs led him to a hallway with two doors on each side and a larger door at the end of the hall. Luckily, he didn't have to go through any of the doors because the breaker box sat on the wall by the large door.

The door itself was made from the same material as the front entryway, but like the key, it had two triangles carved on it. A circle of strange symbols surrounded the triangles. They looked like backward letters and odd shapes, and it made Franklin's head ache to stare at them for too long. Perhaps it was the poor lighting.

Franklin popped the breaker box open. None of the switches looked like they had flipped, but he turned them all off and back on again anyway. He found a light switch next to the door, and when he flipped it on, nothing happened.

He looked around for more breakers but couldn't find anything. However, conduit from the box climbed alongside the door and through the wall. Maybe there was another box on the other side.

Franklin tried the door, but it wouldn't open. He couldn't find a keyhole anywhere; instead, he found a keypad. It must have been one of those fancy cipher locks.

Franklin pulled out his phone and tried to call his boss. It went straight to voicemail. Instead, he sent a text to the strange number.

What's the code for the basement door? I need to get to the other breaker box.

Ryker watched in horror as the signal dropped to 23%. A warning popped up on his screen showing the lab's logo of two triangles spinning in circles. Beneath the logo in bold, flashing letters was:

WARNING: CROSS-DIMENSIONAL SPILLAGE DETECTED. FIND THE NEAREST SECURED SHELTER!

Ryker tried the door to the lab again, but it had been sealed shut. The acrid stink of burnt metal told him they had welded the doors closed. It was a tomb now. A tomb for him and for...

He glanced over to the clearsteel tube. A shadowy mass of ropy tendrils explored the inside of the tube. He couldn't even see the human body in there anymore.

However, if they could complete the objective, it would send the borer back to its plane of existence. Then they would have to let him out. Right? He'd be a hero and maybe even get a day off.

Another message popped up in his queue. It was from the subject.

Ryker opened it up.

34%334st t3e code for th@ do%r

Oh, thank God. They were closer than ever to finishing the objective.

He typed a reply and hit send.

The signal dropped to 20%, and the clearsteel tube cracked.

Franklin's phone buzzed with a reply.

343799. Get it done ASAP!

Franklin put the code into the door. The deadbolt unlocked with a mechanical whir. Franklin pushed the door open, and the house exhaled stale air in his face.

The conduit led down a hallway to another set of metal doors. As Franklin made his way toward the doors, his steps echoed in the sterile enclosure. He neared the doors, and they slid open on their own, revealing a circular room.

The outer edge was all stonework and natural, as if the builders had burrowed into the bedrock. Franklin paused on that word, burrowed. He wasn't sure why he thought that or why the word itself wouldn't leave the tip of his tongue.

Framed pictures lined the wall at various intervals. Franklin got close to one of the pictures and shined his light on it.

The picture was on some sort of tan medium, maybe leather or something similar. The familiar two-triangle symbol was burned into the leather, but two wavy lines connected these triangles.

The next picture depicted a circle with a diagonal line burned into it, like a warning or a no trespassing sign. Underneath the circle sat a symbol that looked like a tree.

The next one made his stomach roll. The leather was slightly different in color. It was lighter than the others. Yet, like the others, it had an odd symbol burned into it: a lightning bolt running through a mountain. However, off-center from it all was a human nipple.

The leather was human skin. They were all human skin.

He turned to leave, but the center of the room lit up with harsh fluorescent lighting. Plexiglass separated Franklin from the center. Inside was a large triangle drawn into the floor in a rusty brown color. However, that wasn't what made Franklin throw up.

A person was tied to the chair in the middle of the triangle. It was skeletal, its skin stretched tight across its bones. Franklin couldn't tell if it was a man or a woman, or even if it was still alive. A section of skin on the person's thigh was missing as if it had been flayed away. He guessed by the state of it that it wasn't. But he still inched towards the plexiglass and tapped.

"Hello?"

If it heard him, it didn't respond.

Franklin walked around the circle, looking for any signs of life. Dozens of holes showed on the person's back. The skin was red and puckered as if things had burst out of its body.

Burrowed.

All over the floor were hundreds of dried-up black *things* that looked like worms or snakes, or maybe eels. It was hard to say in their desiccated state.

It made his skin crawl. He absentmindedly scratched at his arm and felt something wriggle under the skin.

Franklin turned his attention to his arm. Just under his fingers, something long, about four inches, writhed. It pushed against his skin from the inside, creating a black shadow before burrowing back into the muscle.

Pain shot up his arm, and his fingers began to twitch involuntarily. He screamed and dug at his arm with his fingers, quickly tearing through the skin and drawing blood. As he dug, it brushed past his digits, slick with its own secretions and his blood. He grabbed and pulled.

Inch by inch it came free, squirming between his fingers until he pulled it out with a pop. Blood flew into the air, and the thing squealed with a high-pitched scream as it tried to gain purchase on his body again. It was black and pulsed with a deep purple glow. It had no eyes or legs, but it did have a mouth with hundreds of tiny, translucent teeth.

Franklin flung it to the ground and stomped it with his boot. Yellowish goo spurted out and coated the stone floor. Some of it hit the plexiglass wall, and when it did, the wall slid down into the earth.

Exposed to the elements, the body began to rapidly decompose, and the stench hit Franklin in the face. He gagged but somehow kept from throwing up. Pain lanced through his legs, and he fell to his knees. Something crawled under his cheek and down his neck. At the same time, two of the things burst through his back and screamed as they ate through his shirt.

Franklin stumbled forward, and his hand brushed against a large knife made out of obsidian. He hadn't noticed it before, but now it was in his hands.

Franklin had seen this knife before. He knew it. Something in his blood spoke to the natural blade. The handle was made from bone. The bones of his ancestors.

The knife pulsed in his hand as if it had a heartbeat of its own. Franklin dropped to his knees, and blood poured from his nostrils onto the floor. The stones ate the blood, sucking it dry, and the room took on the same beat as the knife.

The figure in the chair let out a dusty gasp. Its eyes flashed open in a wide, painful look. It scanned the room until it found Franklin. The skin on its face began to ripple as dozens of those worms crawled underneath.

It screamed.

Franklin screamed.

Alarms blared to life in the lab, and Ryker couldn't keep up with all the incoming data. Streams of numbers, symbols, and letters scrolled across his screen, almost in a blur. The thing in the tube slammed itself on the inside wall over and over in an attempt to break free.

If they failed their objective, if the signal dropped to zero, they'd lose contact, and it would be all over.

The crack in the clearsteel tube spider-webbed across its length.

Then, a piece of the clearsteel broke free and fell to the floor with a dull clank. Ryker stood from his desk and stumbled back towards the door as a length of slimy tentacle pushed through the break. The end of the of it split and revealed rows of daggerlike teeth as it emitted a high-pitched shriek.

His monitor flashed red.

The signal was at 6%.

"Come on! Finish the objective!"

He tried the door one more time although he knew it was sealed shut. There just wasn't anything else to do.

Franklin's vision blurred. The runes and sigils in the framed swatches of flesh emitted an orange glow. Whispers from everywhere and nowhere squirmed into his ears.

Finish it.

Do your part.

Take your place.

Franklin tore his shirt off. Hundreds of tiny wounds that wept tears of black blood were on his chest. The wounds turned into tiny mouths that matched the worms and they screamed and laughed and cried.

His heart felt like it was going to burst as a massive worm slithered through his ribs, ripping the meat between them and crushing cartilage. He cried out and fell to the floor.

Franklin's legs kicked and shuddered as his arms flopped around. He couldn't control his body as the thing swam through his tissue. It pushed up his neck and windpipe, and he couldn't breathe.

Then it reversed direction and slithered back down past his lungs to his stomach and stopped moving.

Franklin lay on the ground heaving as sweat poured off his body. He could barely move but managed to get to his elbows and knees. He coughed up huge wads of the black, viscous, blood that burned as it passed through his esophagus.

Two feet showed up in front of him. They were blackened and twisted with rot. He looked up and came face-to-face with the person who had been sitting in the chair. Stringy hair covered his face, but two dark pits where his eyes had been moments before stared into Franklin's soul.

Two of the eelworms wriggled out from its sockets and fell to the floor. The person smiled at him and pointed with a bony finger.

It held the knife in the other hand. "Finish it."

Franklin grabbed the knife. The thing in his chest began to swim again, but he stabbed the obsidian blade into his guts. The skin blistered and burned where it touched the blade. The knife hit the worm, and ginger-colored goo spilled out, mixing with the blood that poured from the wound.

"Got you," Franklin said through grit teeth.

He wrenched the blade up, enlarging the wound, screaming in agony. When the cut was large enough, he shoved a hand in and grabbed the worm. It was slick and he had trouble keeping hold of it. Yet he pulled, and it came out, bit by bit.

The worm convulsed and tried to burrow deeper. More pain flared up his chest and took Franklin's breath away.

He dropped the knife and grabbed the thing with both hands, pulling with all the strength he had left. Finally, it gave, and Franklin gagged as it slid out of his guts. The thing screamed at him and tried to bite his face.

Its screams made the other smaller worms in his body go nuts as hundreds of the things crawled and bit. Franklin dropped the thing on the floor and it slithered away. His intestines spilled out from his wound and hit the floor with a wet plop.

Franklin fell to the ground. Time slowed down for him, and all he could hear was the slow beat of his heart. With each pump, it became slower and quieter.

A cold claw of a hand touched his shoulder, and for a moment the worms from it mingled with the worms burrowing out of Franklin's back. Then came the raspy whisper of the person who had been in the chair.

"You're not done yet. Oh no. You have an objective to complete."

Franklin somehow had the knife again. He sat up and looked down at his chest. It was hard to focus on anything, and all he wanted to do was close his eyes and let oblivion take him. But there was an itch. An itch he had to scratch.

He took the knife to his chest and began to carve.

Ryker watched the signal strength degrade to 1%. Then it held. The flashing alarms stopped, and the lab's harsh white light flickered back to life.

A green message appeared on the screen.

OBJECTIVE COMPLETE

"Thank the gods!"

The borer let out a final screech before it fell onto the floor. It flopped around several times before orange goo seeped out of its body and it deflated.

He ran over to the intercom. "It's done, you can let me out now!"

The speaker crackled to life.

Negative. There is a new objective.

A small door in the lab opened, and a new clearsteel tube slid in. The tube opened, expelling air and sterile spray in all directions.

No! He had done his duty and ensured the objective was met! They were supposed to let him out!

He hit the intercom button again, but the familiar click of it engaging didn't occur. He hit it several more times, but nobody answered.

The computer monitor flashed with a new message.

AWAITING VIABLE SUBJECT.

Ryker looked at the clearsteel tube and then shuffled over. Tears fell from his eyes as he touched its surface. The metal was warmer than he thought it would be.

"Do I have to?"

Ryker took his clothes off. He folded them neatly and placed them on the nearby desk. Then he crawled into the tube. The inside stretched for eons, and like a worm, he burrowed.

"Home"

She had curled up in the corner of our ramshackle cabin, a tattered wool blanket wrapped around her body like a grey cocoon. It reminded me of when she was a child. Small murmurs and cries slipped through her lips as she slept. Maybe she felt what was wrong with me on a subconscious level, or maybe it was just a bad dream.

I didn't want to leave her all alone. A part of me knew she was old enough to take care of herself. A part of me didn't care. I didn't want to leave.

I almost didn't.

Yet it was that kind of thinking that would lead to her dying horribly and probably by my hand. My fingers brushed the bandage around my arm, and the pain was motivation enough to get moving.

We only had one gun between the two of us with a handful of shells. She would need it more than me, so it was a parting gift.

I didn't leave a note. I didn't say goodbye. Going through those motions would only make me weak. She wouldn't agree with what I was doing, but hopefully, she would at least understand. We'd seen too many good people turn, and she didn't need to add me to that list. I blew her a kiss and left.

The wind outside howled across the barren landscape, burning my chapped skin, and making it almost impossible to maneuver without goggles. Unfortunately, my only pair were scratched and blemished to the point that they were almost unserviceable. Better than nothing since the alternative was going blind.

Although this would be my last journey, I had a purpose, and it wasn't to wander aimlessly until I turned to bone and sand like everything else in this godforsaken landscape. I was going home.

My family had owned a small plot of land up Sardine Canyon in the small town of Mantua, overlooking a large pond that thought it was a lake. When I was younger, I couldn't wait to get out of town. Once everything started to wilt and burn, people couldn't get out fast enough.

Red clouds churned in the sky, casting the land below in a rust-tinged shadow accentuated by the occasional blast of lightning. It made it difficult to judge the sun's position. The pain throbbing up my arm was enough to tell me I was a dead man walking. However, that didn't mean I wanted to get torn to pieces caught in the dark.

The wind and dust made it hard to navigate, and I had to keep the mountains to my right, using them as a guiding line to the canyon. It wasn't much longer until mountains opened, showing me the way to Mantua. A few more miles up a broken stretch of asphalt and I'd be home.

The hills crept along either side of me as I made my way into the canyon. I was lost in thought staring at dead trees lining the road when pain lanced up my arm. My lungs refused to work, and after several agonizing moments, I dropped to my knees and hacked up a wad of black tar that scratched my throat to shreds on the way up. I wiped my face with a ragged scarf and was about to stand up when something moved in the gravel behind me.

"You left."

It was her.

"You shouldn't have followed me."

It wasn't my voice anymore. It was tinny and jagged, like the voice of one of *them*.

She didn't say anything but helped me to my feet. Her flaxen hair floated around her dirty, tear-streaked face like wispy tendrils. The world turned upside down, and I almost fell over again, but she caught me.

I hugged her, partly to steady myself, and partly to hold her close one last time. She trembled in my arms, her soft sobs muffled against my chest.

"You don't have to do this," she said, her voice trembling and quiet. She knew what would happen—what *was* happening.

Her purity was a stench, like rotten meat. I had an urge to rip it out of her, piece by little piece.

"You have to go, honey. It's getting worse."

"I don't want to."

Tears streamed down her face in tiny tributaries, blazing new trails through the dirt. I had no idea when it would get dark. That's when they would come for her—when I would turn on her.

"Go. Before it's too late."

I gave her a kiss on the forehead, resisting the temptation to sink my teeth into her soft cheek. We shared one last embrace and then I left her for the second time. I didn't look behind me, but the weight of her eyes was heavy on my back.

I rounded the bend, and Mantua came into view. It was as I feared. The small town had burnt to its foundation, the small lake nothing more than a stagnant pool. Up the hill sat my family's land. Like the rest of the town, the house had burned in the purge; however, part of the structure was still intact.

I had started up the hill when a gunshot rang out in the distance, stopping me in my tracks. Two more followed shortly thereafter, echoing through the hills. Then, it went silent.

I tried to imagine she was okay, but nothing was okay in this world, not anymore.

The sun was setting, and as the light receded past the mountaintops, the whispering started. I couldn't understand what they were saying, but as I neared my old house, and as it got darker and darker, the whispers became more and more clear.

They were welcoming me home.

"The Other Inside Me"

When I look in the mirror, I see myself most of the time, and there is nothing to worry about. However, there are times I see someone else. They have my eyes. My facial structure. They even move when I do. But I know what I'm looking at isn't me.

I know it can't be me because when I see the other's image reflected in the mirror, I hate how their body looks. I hate their beard and how they dress!

Then, there are days when I look in the mirror and see the same image as before, but now it feels right. It's those days that I begin to question my sanity. Was what I felt before true, or was it just a strange phase?

But I know the truth. There's somebody else inside me, fighting to get out and getting stronger every day.

There are times when I can feel them, but I go about my day anyway. When I try and suppress the other, they remind me of my foolishness. They call me an imposter.

It was silly to think I could find victory by fighting myself. The only way forward is to embrace the other inside me.

Besides... we are stronger together.

"Night of the Wormheads"

Roger sped down the dark two-lane highway back to Thatcher. Thatcher was a tiny little town situated in the foothills of the Wasatch Mountains in Utah. Other than ranching and farming, there weren't many opportunities for a graduating high school student. He couldn't wait to graduate and get the hell out of town. He was well over the speed limit, but the snow was starting to fall, and he wanted to get back before it got worse.

The night sky lit up with a brilliant ball of light. At first, he thought maybe it was an airplane, but it was coming down too fast.

And it was on fire. It had to be a meteor.

The ball flew over his truck, coming so close it rattled the dashboard. He hit the brakes and fishtailed on the slick roads before sliding off onto the gravel shoulder. Roger craned his neck and looked behind him as the ball rocketed past the hill. Seconds later, a huge gout of orange flame burst from where the thing had hit.

All thoughts of football scholarships flew from his mind, replaced with thoughts of finding a meteor. How much could someone get for getting one those? He hoped it was six digits or more.

Roger turned his truck around and hit the old dirt road that would take him over the rise. He crept up the road, bouncing and rocking as he went until he crested the hill.

Burning trees and brush marked the place where the thing had come rolling in. About two hundred yards away, a small crater glowed with smoldering embers and pale white light. Roger hit the gas and drove as fast as he could, but halfway there, his truck sputtered and died.

The radio went nuts with horrible static squeal. He tried to lower the volume, but it didn't help. It wouldn't turn off either. Finally, he gave up and hopped out of the truck.

Roger jogged up to the crater. Bits of trees and shrubs smoldered all around it, and steam rose into the air from the heat. The blast had thrown dirt and debris all over the road and nearby field and even took out one of Old Man McCormick's cows. He was going to be pissed! That man loved his cows more than his wife.

The air was downright hot near the meteor. It felt more like a summer night than a frigid winter one.

Roger didn't know what he expected to see—maybe a huge ball of rock, metal, and crystal, shining in colors he couldn't even imagine. However, sitting in the center of the crater was a small metal sphere about the size of a basketball. Roger expected something as large as a car. How had this tiny thing cause so much damage? It pulsed with a pale white light similar to a full moon. Roger moved closer, reached out, and tapped the sphere. He expected it to be hot, but it was cold to the touch. He picked it up. The sphere was heavier than it looked. As far as he could tell, it didn't have any markings.

Still, it came from space and wasn't natural.

It was going to make him rich.

The same screeching from the radio happened again, only louder. It seemed to come from everywhere and nowhere. Roger's ears rang, and it got so loud it started to hurt. He tried to drop the sphere and cover his ears, but his fingers stuck to the metal. His hands tingled as he tried to pull away.

The pulsing light increased in speed and brightness with each flash.

Soon, there was nothing but light and pain.

Sheriff Rosa Morales sat in a worn-out booth at the Pancake Stop Diner across from her twelve-year old son, David. The diner was dirty and worn down, but it had the best damn coffee in a fifty-mile radius. So, when Judith came by with a fresh pot and asked if Rosa wanted more, she didn't even hesitate.

"Gonna snow tonight," Judith said.

Judith smelled like an ashtray, but Rosa didn't mind. She took a sip of coffee and winced as the hot liquid hit her tongue. "Yeah, sure is. Supposed to be a bad one too."

"Hope it doesn't ruin the festival."

Rosa nodded. The annual Thatcher Lights Festival was a huge deal for the town. It had been going strong for over seventy-five years. She was sure a blizzard wouldn't ruin that tradition.

David looked up from his phone at the mention of the festival. The boy had been looking forward to it for months now because he was supposed to spend a few hours with his father there.

Rosa didn't want to get in the way of that, and she hoped that the weather wouldn't, either. Her marriage had started off like a fairytale, and for ten years it stayed that way. However, her husband's work took him away from the family often, and soon that fairytale turned into a nightmare. They had tried to make it work for David's sake, but they soon realized the healthiest option was divorce. Regardless of how Rosa felt about the man, David needed the time with his father.

"Don't worry, bud, I'm sure it will be fine," Rosa said.

David didn't say anything but buried himself back into the phone. She was worried about him, but from what she had seen, it was normal for kids his age, hell even adults, to find solace in the digital world.

Judith stared out the window for a bit and then shook her head. "Can I get you anything else? Or anything for you, young man?"

David looked at her and shook his head. "No, ma'am. Thank you."

Rosa smiled.

David turned his attention back to the phone and frowned. He tapped the screen a few times and then let the device drop to the table.

"What's up?" Rosa asked.

"No signal."

"Probably just the storm."

She pulled her phone out of her pocket and found it was also searching for service.

The low wail of a fire truck siren grabbed her attention. Rosa looked out the window just in time to catch the red Thatcher Fire Department engine speed past with its lights flashing.

"What's that all about?" Judith asked.

Rosa didn't answer. She had just finished her shift and turned her radio off before coming into the diner. She reached down and twisted the volume knob. The radio blared to life with an intense blast of static.

She flipped through a couple of different channels, but they all had the same, ear-piercing wail. Rosa turned it off.

"Well, guess I'm back on it," she said.

"But what about the festival and Dad?"

"Don't worry, bud. I'll drop you off first."

Judith held up the pot. "Want one for the road?"

"Do you even have to ask?"

David hopped in the front seat of her cruiser. Rosa tried her cell again, but it still didn't have any service.

She drove to Mills Park. It was the only park in town and the location of the Lights Festival. A giant pine tree grew in the center of the park, and every year the town would decorate it with thousands of lights. People brought their own trees to decorate and placed them all around the park.

There were already tons of townsfolk in the park. Some were wandering around looking at the trees while others were putting the final touches on their displays. The town would vote on whose tree was best, and the winner would receive a special ornament to show they had won.

Rosa pulled into the parking lot.

"There he is!" David pointed across the lot.

Rosa followed his finger and found David's father getting out of his beat-up Bronco. She pulled up next to it and David opened the door.

"Hey! Where's my kiss?" Rosa asked.

David sighed loudly and threw his head back in mock despair. "Fine!" He leaned over and kissed her once on the cheek before exploding out of the police cruiser.

"Dad!"

"Hey, kiddo!"

David ran up to his father and hugged him.

Rosa got out of the car and walked over. "John."

John nodded her direction. "Looks like it's going to come down."

Small talk. That's all they ever had these days. It was probably for the best because anything deeper always led to an argument.

"Yep. Hey if it gets too crazy, take him to your place and I'll pick him up, okay?"

"Of course."

"David, you mind your father, got it?"

David nodded, his smile already fading. Kids were uncanny when it came to reading moods.

Rosa didn't want to ruin his night, so she cut it short. "Well, I'm back to work. See you later tonight, buddy."

"Okay, Mom."

As she got back into the cruiser, David and John made their way toward the festival. She watched them for a few more seconds and then headed to the station.

As she pulled up, Deputy Harris was just pulling out. Rosa hit her lights and let the siren blip to get his attention.

"Sheriff, thank god!" Harris said.

He was a young man, fresh from training. He hadn't even been with the department a full year yet. Rosa liked him though because he had keen attention to detail and was self-motivated. "What's going on?"

"Something fell out of the sky just outside of town. Started a fire over at McCormick's Ranch. Messed up our radios though—we can't get any signal through at all."

The first few flakes of snow began to fall. They were light and fluffy, but they were big. Rosa had been around Thatcher long enough to know it was indeed going to be a bad one. "Okay, you lead the way."

Harris nodded and hit the street. Rosa followed behind. The snow was already sticking to everything. It wouldn't be long before it covered the roads and made driving hazardous. She hoped the situation wasn't too crazy and that they could all get back before the storm got worse. But as her grandfather used to tell her, hope in one hand and shit in the other, and see which one filled up first. She missed him.

The snow was falling hard by the time they turned onto the dirt road and drove up the hill. A fireman in his protective gear came running down the road, waving his hands and motioning them to stop.

Rosa slowed the cruiser and rolled down her window. "What's up?"

As the fireman got closer, she could see it was Bill Shaughnessy. He was a nice enough man, always professional.

"Howdy, Sheriff. You want to stop right here. Something up the road is messing with our vehicles. Kills 'em."

Rosa looked past him. The fire engine and one of the FD ambulances were about 100 yards up the road. No lights, no sirens, nothing.

"That's weird."

"Tell me about it," Bill said. "Radios are fried too. The only reason we knew about it was because McCormick drove into the station to tell us his ranch was on fire."

Rosa got out of the cruiser and zipped her coat up. It was getting colder by the minute, and she wished she had brought some warmer clothes. Deputy Harris got out as well, and they made their way up the road with Bill in the lead.

The warm glow of a fire lit up the night sky ahead of them. Firefighters worked as a team to get the hose out and start spraying down the field. Some cows grazed nearby, watching the excitement with a lazy look in their eyes.

Up ahead was an old beat-up pickup truck in front of the fire engine.

Rosa tapped Harris on the shoulder and pointed at the truck. "Hey, isn't that Donna's son's truck?"

"Not sure, Boss."

"Hey, Bill! What's up with the truck? Did you find someone out there?"

"No, we didn't. Best guess is that whatever killed our vehicles did the same to that pickup. Maybe the owner decided to try and hoof it out on foot."

"Did you pass anyone on the way up?" Rosa asked.

"Negative."

It didn't make sense. The closest place was Thatcher, which meant they should have crossed paths with anyone walking back. With the way the weather was hitting, it wasn't the time to be out on foot.

"What caused this?"

Bill shrugged. "Not sure. Maybe one of those space rocks or a satellite or something."

This whole situation didn't sit well with Rosa. She didn't like half-assed guesses and theories. Especially when there was a possible missing person out in the snow.

"Harris, follow me."

Rosa walked past the firefighters toward what looked like a crater in the ground. As they neared it, an awful stench of burning hair and raw sewage hit her nose.

"Good lord, what is that?" Harris asked.

Rosa covered her mouth and nose, but it did little to keep the stink out. She opted not to reply so she wouldn't have to taste it as well.

She stepped up to the edge of the crater and almost threw up.

There was a metal sphere that was open and empty. However, that wasn't what made her knees shake. Lying next to the open container was a bloody pile of clothing and hair. She recognized a letterman jacket from the high school. The smell was rancid. It took Rosa back to when her grandpa had shown her how to gut and skin a deer, only it was on a roadkill deer that had been dead most of the day.

The hair was matted with viscera and blood. It was still all together, like it was a wig or something. Then she realized, it was a scalp.

Rosa crouched and grabbed a nearby stick, doing her best not to throw up. There was something underneath the jacket and she couldn't quite see it. She used the stick to move the jacket away. Something wet caught the shine of Harris's flashlight. She poked the stick down, hooked whatever it was, and lifted.

At first, she thought it was more clothing or a rag, but the texture wasn't right. Then it lazily spun on the end of the stick and revealed a face. A human face that looked like a macabre mask.

She found Donna's kid.

Rosa sped back to Thatcher as fast as she dared in the snowstorm. She had to let the mayor know and get everyone home. There was a deranged killer on the loose. Deputy Harris was on his way to round up the other deputies. They were going to need all hands on deck for this one.

As she sped down the road, something caught her eye. Dozens of cows were lying in the field next to the fence. Yet, something was off about them. They should have been much bigger. These cows appeared almost deflated.

Rosa hit the brakes and slid to a stop. She hopped out of the cruiser and made her way over to the cows. It wasn't cold enough to kill cattle, but the snow was coming down thick. By the time she got over to the herd, there was already a fine blanket of white covering their black hides.

Whatever had happened to them, it had happened recently; otherwise, they would have been so covered with snow she wouldn't have seen them at all.

Rosa drew her pistol as she walked over. The stink of viscera hit her nose as she neared. The cows were only guts and hide. The bodies were gone.

Stranger yet were dozens of bloody cow tracks and a set of human tracks, shoeless at that, all heading toward Thatcher.

Judith stepped out back and stood by the dumpster to cut some of the wind. She pulled a pack of smokes from her pocket and fished her lighter out. It was frigid outside, but her smoke breaks were ritual. If she missed one, well, it was just best not to talk about what would happen.

Judith put a cigarette between her lips and lit it with the lighter, thanking anyone listening that it lit on the first go. She took a drag and almost sighed as the smoke went down into her lungs.

The new cook stepped out with a bag full of garbage. Judith couldn't remember his name—Ben or Jake, or something like that.

He walked past, scratching his belly with one hand. As he opened the dumpster and threw the garbage in, he cast a sidelong glance her way. "Those things will be the death of you."

Judith rolled her eyes and took another drag. "Like I've never heard that before."

He shrugged and walked back into the diner. Judith leaned against the dumpster and played through several scenarios in her head where she told off Ben or Jake or Chad or whoever he was. She missed the old cook. At least he minded his business.

Her ears started to ring and the wind picked up. Judith took a final pull on the cigarette and then flicked it away so she could cover her ears. It was almost like a dog whistle or something, like fingers against a chalkboard. She could hardly stand it.

Judith made her way back towards the diner, but a series of strange white lights shone on the other side of the wooden fence that separated the diner from the nearby field. She crept closer to the fence and peeked through a hole.

Dozens of figures crawled in the snow. They looked like sick cows, but wrong. They were thin, wiry, and walked in jerky motions. Yet that wasn't their strangest feature. The oddest thing was the wriggling mass of worms sprouting from their hairless faces that glowed like fluorescent light bulbs.

A bright light lit up behind her. She turned and found herself face to face with a skinless man dripping blood onto the snow-covered ground. His face was nothing more than a mass of the same glowing worms.

She screamed as he grabbed her by the shoulders and pulled her close. The worms burrowed into her face, and all that was left was light.

Rosa tried to call David, but the cell service was nonexistent. She growled and threw her phone into the passenger seat and drove faster. Rosa had to make sure David was safe and get to the mayor. They'd both be at the festival.

Even though the snow was getting crazy, the park was packed with people. The center tree was lit, casting a dazzling display of red, green, and blue lights into the air. The snow caught the lights' reflection and created a beautiful show.

She pulled up to the curb and got out of the cruiser. The delightful smell of funnel cakes, fried food, and hot chocolate wafted in the air. But the stench of death still permeated her mouth, and eating or drinking was the last thing on her mind.

Rosa scanned the crowd looking for David's blue winter jacket. However, the number of people all wearing heavy coats, the snow falling in droves, and the lights made trying to find him difficult.

She walked through the crowd and called out his name. Finally, she found him. He was over next to a tree decorated with fake icicles and silver tinsel.

"David!" Rosa ran over there and grabbed him by the shoulder.

David screamed and spun around, and Rosa's heart fell. It wasn't David at all.

It was a teenage girl wearing the same coat, her eyes wide with fright.

The girl's mom grabbed her and pulled her close. "What the hell, Sheriff?"

Rosa put her hands up. "Sorry! I thought she was someone else. But hey, you need to pack up and get home fast. It's not safe out here."

The woman didn't say anything but moved her kid over to the next tree away from Rosa. Rosa sighed and started searching the crowd again. She didn't see David, but she did see the mayor.

Mayor Young was an older gentleman with a salt-and-pepper beard and wispy hair. He had a runner's frame and liked to boast that he could outdistance anyone in town.

She jogged over to him and waved to get his attention.

"Ah, Sheriff Morales, how are you this fine evening?" The mayor's voice was deep and gravelly.

"Not good. Look, we have a situation."

The mayor raised an eyebrow. "Oh, what's that? Have we run out of hot chocolate already?"

He chuckled and the crowd of townspeople standing beside him joined in.

"No. Can I speak to you in private please?"

The mayor's face darkened, but only for an instant before it was back to his usual, jovial visage. "Of course. Please excuse me while I speak with our fine law enforcement professional."

Rosa led the mayor behind the nearby food truck. As soon as they were out of sight from the crowd the mayor's smile turned into a frown. "What's wrong with you? You can't come here and start talking like that. You'll scare these people half to death."

"We've got a killer on the loose. You need to get these people home."

Mayor Young furrowed his brow. "What do you mean we have a killer on the loose?"

Rosa explained the situation and what she had seen. Mayor Young listened, but as soon as she was finished, he huffed and rolled his eyes. "Look, I'm not canceling our festival and getting everyone riled up because you found a dead body. It could be a bear or some wild animal."

"It wasn't a wild animal. Trust me on that. No wild animal could do what I saw."

"Your area of expertise is law enforcement, not animal attacks."

"And your area of expertise is *supposed* to be the well-being of this town and its residents!"

His face flushed red. "I suggest you watch what you say and how you say it. Don't forget who you are speaking to. Keep it up and I'll suspend you without pay."

Rosa bit her tongue to stop what she wanted to say next. She couldn't believe her ears.

Screw it! The town's safety was paramount.

Before she could say what she wanted to say, a scream cut through the night.

Rosa ran around the food truck to see. More screams followed, and Rosa ran toward them, hoping and praying to anything that would listen that it wasn't David.

As she pushed her way through a fleeing throng of people, a loud buzzing hit her ears. It was like a dentist's drill but worse. Rosa finally shouldered past the last person and blanched at what she found.

Two human-sized figures stood side-by-side. Exposed muscle and fatty tissue glistened under the lights of the nearby trees. However, these beings emitted their own light from a mass of writhing worms that sprouted from their face.

Each one held a citizen of Thatcher in their arms. The worms stretched from their faces and attached themselves to their victims, who convulsed violently.

Rosa drew her sidearm. "Stop! Drop them now!"

If the things heard her, they didn't show any sign.

More screaming came from the side. Rosa glanced that direction and found what looked like a herd of cattle, similarly skinned and each with their own glowing face worms. The herd stampeded into a crowd of spectators. As the cattle knocked people over, the worms struck like vipers.

One cow ran straight for Rosa. She aimed and shot. The bullet struck the cow in the forehead and it crumpled to the ground. It opened its mouth wide, wider than should have been possible, and a bright white light shot up into the night sky. The thing screamed so loud Rosa thought her eardrums would burst.

She shot two more times. The bullets hit and the screaming stopped as the white light flew out of the cow's mouth and up into clouds. The worms wriggled a few more times then lay still. Seconds later, they dimmed and went dark.

One of the human things dropped its victim. The vic was Tom, who ran the hardware store. He yelled in pain, his eyes bulging from their sockets. Ropy tendrils squirmed just under the skin on his face. He reached out to Rosa and tried to say something, but only a loud screech came from his mouth. Then, the worms burst through his skin and he flopped in the snow like a fish out of water. He reached up with his hands and began to tear his skin and clothes away until he was a bloody mess of writhing worms.

The thing that had originally attacked Tom came running at Rosa. She brought her gun up and put two rounds center mass. The bullets ripped into the thing, but it kept coming.

Rosa adjusted her aim and planted a round into its head. It fell to the ground only a few feet away and flailed about until, just like the cow, a burst of light flew into the air. It was dead.

Rosa turned and ran. More and more townsfolk fell to the glowing worms' assault, only to get up as one of them. People ran in all directions, their screams mixed in with the loud screeching.

Then, a voice cut through the cacophony.

"Mom!"

Rosa turned toward the big tree and found David and John in a mass of people. John had an arm around David to keep him close. Rosa ran towards them.

So too did three skinless wormheads.

One of the wormheads jumped toward David but missed and hit an elderly man beside them. John wrenched David away from the thing and kicked it in the ribs. It let out a screech and tore itself away from the old man, taking chunks of the man's face with it.

David screamed as John put himself between the creature and the boy and pulled a pocket knife from his belt.

Rosa didn't have a good line of fire. If she missed, she'd hit John, David, or one of the dozen other bystanders. She ran as fast as she could.

She was almost there when something slammed into her from behind and pulled her to the ground. Rosa rolled to her back and kicked on instinct. Her boot impacted something soft, and when she looked down, a dozen of the glowing worms were trying to burrow their way through the thick leather of her shoe.

She kicked again, knocking the creature up onto its knees. Rosa pointed and shot straight through its mouth. It screamed and died. Another wormhead jumped into the air towards her.

Time slowed for Rosa. She pointed the pistol and shot but missed. The glowing worms stretched and wriggled towards her as the thing fell. Just as it was about to land on her, John tackled it from the side.

The thing let out a screech and fought him. John stabbed it with his knife over and over. The thing's tentacles grabbed his arm, and he screamed in pain as they bit into his flesh. Rosa rolled to her side and put a bullet through its skull.

The tentacles dropped away from John's arm and he fell to the ground clutching it with his good hand. Rosa crawled over to him as David ran over.

"Dad! Are you okay?"

John sat up. "Stay back!"

David stopped short of John and shuffled from foot to foot. Rosa got up and ran over to David, hugging him close. After an intense embrace, she inspected him for wounds.

"I'm okay, Mom," he said and shrugged away. "I'm okay."

Rosa pulled him close again and kissed him. Then she turned to John. "Thank you."

He nodded and tried to stand. Rosa helped him to his feet.

"Mom!"

David pointed over to the food truck where six of the worm creatures had the Mayor surrounded. He tried to run, but they pounced on him at the same time, and his screams echoed through the night.

"We have to go. Come on!" Rosa said.

The three of them ran towards the parking lot as fast as they could. The screeching got louder as the things closed in. John's breathing became labored and he stumbled.

Rosa pushed David towards the car. "Go!" And then she turned to John.

She helped him to his feet, but after two more steps, he stopped.

"Get out of here," he said through his teeth.

"No, we can make it!"

"No, *we* can't. But you can." He looked at her and something crawled under his skin just below his eye. "Now go."

Rosa backed away.

"Dad?"

John looked past Rosa. "I love you, kiddo." Then he turned and ran back towards the throng of worm creatures.

"Dad, no!"

David ran past Rosa, but she grabbed him and held him tight. He struggled to get loose but couldn't get away. John tackled the first of the incoming worm creatures and the rest surrounded him.

Rosa turned David away from the scene and led him to the cruiser. She got in, fired the engine on, and sped away as David slammed his hands against the window and yelled for his father.

As they drove down the road, David cried in the passenger seat. She reached over and pulled him close, and he hugged her and sobbed against her chest.

The tall pine of Mills Park got smaller in the rearview, its lights mixed with the glow coming from the wormheads. With the falling snow, it was quite a sight. On any other occasion, it would have been beautiful.

As it stood, Rosa would be happy if she never saw another holiday light again.

"The Old Oak"

Every morning on the way to school, Bailey would walk to the Old Oak, sit at the base of its trunk, and listen. They swore they heard things coming from deep within the tree's core—whispers and promises that things would be better, and even hints of a song. Perhaps it was just Bailey's mind playing tricks, but they liked to think it was real.

Bailey didn't know how long the oak had stood, but they knew it was ancient. It was just a feeling, something deep down in their gut. Perhaps it was the sheer size of the tree, towering above the others in the forest like a god. Or perhaps it was the strange shapes and figures Bailey could see when they stared at the bark. One shape stood out from the rest. It was a swirl with what appeared to maybe be antlers or branches. The longer they stared at it, the harder it was to focus on the strange shape.

Regardless, Bailey loved that oak, and they knew the Old Oak loved them back. They had a strange connection.

From the moment they had found the oak, they knew it was there for them.

Being in the woods, away from other people, was Bailey's happy place. It's where they could be themselves, wear whatever they wanted to, and talk about whatever they wanted to talk about. The Old Oak didn't judge. It accepted them.

That's why the Old Oak was the only thing in Bailey's mind as they ran down the hall of Hill Valley High School as fast as they could.

Bailey was faster than Tommy, and they had a good lead, but the squeak of sneakers on the floor told Bailey that Tommy and his gang of imbeciles weren't too far behind.

Bailey's lungs screamed for air, and their heart threatened to pound through their chest as they sprinted. The doors to the school were just ahead. They hoped Tommy and the others would give up the chase as soon as they were outside, though Bailey knew that probably wouldn't be the case. Bailey had done something terrible.

Bailey had embarrassed Tommy.

It started with the usual bullying. All because a bit of the yellow sunflower print summer dress had fallen out of Bailey's backpack when they pulled their gym clothes out to change for class.

"What the hell is that you fucking faggot?" Tommy yelled, pointing at the dress.

Tommy played the stereotypical jock too well. He was athletic, the girls loved him, the teachers put up with his bullshit, but he was cruel and liked to pick on Bailey and others he deemed lesser or *other*.

Bailey tried to stuff the dress back into their bag, but Tommy pushed Bailey down onto the floor and snatched the backpack away. Then, he pulled the dress out and held it up like a trophy for everyone to see.

"Well, isn't this just precious? Doesn't this look cute? What do you think, Dave?" Tommy asked.

Dave had a mustache that looked more like a bad hair implant, but apparently, he was very proud of what little facial hair he could grow. Bailey had overheard him talking one day in math class about how he thought it made him look older. Dave laughed and touched the dress with his hand as if he was inspecting it.

"Yeah, I like the flowers. Too cute. You going to wear this for your first date?" Dave asked.

Bailey's face flushed with heat. They stood and tried to grab the dress. Tommy snatched it away from Bailey's reach. Jeff, Tommy's other right-hand moron, pushed Bailey into the nearby lockers, eliciting an "ooooh" response from the already growing crowd of onlookers.

"Give it back!" Bailey said.

"Why, you going to go wear it after school?" Tommy asked.

Tears welled in Bailey's eyes. They didn't want to cry. It would just make things worse.

"It's my sister's dress; give it back! Please!"

"It's my sister's dress; give it back!" Jeff said, mocking Bailey.

It wasn't a lie, it *was* Charlize's dress, but she had no clue Bailey had taken it from her room. If it got damaged or she found out, it would be way worse than anything Tommy could do. However, Bailey had taken the dress because they liked how it looked on them. They felt comfortable in it and planned to wear it in the woods after school when they had some time to themselves.

The woods were safe. Not like school... or home.

One time they had taken one of Charlize's pink sweaters and a pair of black leggings and wore them in their room. They loved the way it brought out their feminine side. Then, their mom had come home early from work, decided to clean things up, and barged into their room right when Bailey was putting on some lipstick. They had saved up some of their allowance and bought the lipstick at the local drugstore. When they brought it up to the checkout, they shook so bad wondering what the employee would think or say. Bailey even lied and said it was a birthday present for their sister. The checker didn't care one way or the other. The look on Bailey's mother's face was enough to tell them that they couldn't be themselves around her. She never said a thing about it other than telling them to wipe the shit off their face and put the clothes in the laundry, but her tone cut them to the marrow.

"You know, you kind of look like your sister. I bet if you put this pretty dress on, you could be her twin," Tommy said.

"Yeah, make him put it on! Force him out into gym class wearing it!" Dave said, giggling.

The thought froze Bailey's blood. "Please, just give it back."

The tears flowed freely now. Shame, guilt, and fear crept through Bailey's body. Yet, there was something else in the back of their mind—rage. Their hands clenched into fists, nails biting into skin.

Something flipped in Bailey. They were scared for sure, but something else rose inside of them. Something that fed on that rage. Something that empowered them.

Bailey lunged forward and pushed Tommy as hard as they could. Tommy didn't see it coming. It caught him off guard, and he stumbled backward, tripping over the nearby bench and toppling to the ground.

Dave and Jeff didn't know what to do. The crowd of kids started laughing at Tommy. Tommy's face went beet red. His mouth opened and closed like a fish out of water as he stared at the gathering of students.

Bailey ate up Tommy's embarrassment and humility like candy. It sent endorphins running through their entire body, making them feel better than they ever had before.

Bailey picked up the dress and stuffed it back into their backpack. That movement caught Tommy's eyes—his visage switched from embarrassment to pure anger.

"You're fucking dead," Tommy said.

Bailey believed it. They took off running, with Tommy, Jeff, and Dave following close behind, and shouldered through the heavy school doors. The impact stung, but they knew getting caught by Tommy would be far worse.

The sun felt good on their face, and the edge of the forest was only 300 yards away. Bailey knew they would be safe if they could make it there before Tommy caught up with them.

A second later, Tommy burst out of the school. Fear overtook the feeling of power that had previously filled them, and Bailey's confidence wavered. They were halfway to the trees, but their legs started to wobble, and they could hardly breathe anymore.

"Stop running! I'm going to kick your ass!"

There wasn't much motivation to stop with that statement, so Bailey continued to push through the pain and exhaustion and run as fast as their legs would go.

The metallic taste of blood hit their throat, and their lungs burned as they tried to take in more air. Tommy, Jeff, and Dave were almost on top of them.

"You're going to pay for what you did!" Tommy yelled.

The trees were so close now. It was Bailey's bastion, their fortress of solitude, and they knew without a doubt that they would be safe there. Bailey wasn't sure how they knew it, but they knew it to be true deep down in their sinew. They just needed a break.

Jeff's scream made Bailey's ears ring. However, Bailey didn't look back until they made it to the tree line. When they did, they couldn't believe what they saw.

Jeff writhed on the ground, clutching his leg next to a tree root that stuck up from the ground. The bone of his shin stuck through the skin like a jagged tooth. Blood poured from the wound and into the grass.

Tommy and Dave stared in horror at their friend, wondering what to do. Bailey didn't waste any more time. They turned and ran into the woods.

"You piece of shit! I'm going to kill you!" Tommy yelled, though his voice seemed further away, muffled by the trees.

Bailey continued to run until they just couldn't muster the breath anymore. They knew Tommy was more than likely searching for them, but if they tried to run again, they would keel over and die.

Eventually, Bailey found themselves at the base of the Old Oak. They tried to make themselves as small as possible and catch their breath.

They were scared, but the Old Oak gave them comfort. After what felt like forever, Bailey's heart finally started to slow down. Finally, they leaned their head against the trunk of the tree and closed their eyes.

"You get out here, faggot!" Tommy yelled.

Bailey's eyes shot open. They didn't dare move.

"You broke Jeff's leg, you piece of shit!"

That wasn't true at all. It had been a horrible accident, hadn't it? If Tommy and the others had left them alone, none of this would have happened.

A moment later, Tommy busted through the trees. His eyes were wild with rage and hate, and when he saw Bailey, his lips turned into a cruel smile. That smile promised pain.

"You're mine now," Tommy said and stalked toward them like a rabid animal.

"Tommy, calm down. I'm sorry, okay?" Bailey said. They stood, their back against the Old Oak.

"We're *way* past that now."

Tommy stopped to pick up a large branch about the size of a baseball bat. He sneered and gripped the branch with both hands.

"How many swings do you think it will take to decorate that tree with your brains?"

"Tommy, please..."

The tears began to blaze their way down Bailey's cheeks again. They had never seen Tommy like this. They were scared.

Tommy was going to kill them. They knew it deep in their heart, and soon they would just be another depressing statistic.

Bailey thought about running again, but Tommy was close enough now that he would catch them easily. Plus, they just didn't have the energy anymore. They needed help.

The Old Oak groaned. Branches snapped, and the ground shook.

Tommy stopped in his tracks, looking at something above Bailey's head. He dropped the club in his hand and took a step back. A dark, wet stain appeared on his jeans as Tommy pissed his pants.

Something breathed behind Bailey. They could feel the rise and fall of its chest, though nothing but the Old Oak was behind them. Rough-hewn hands with wooden claws and bark for skin touched Bailey's shoulders. Not in a menacing way, but in a protective way.

Bailey should have been scared, but instead, they were relieved. They watched in awe as Tommy turned tail and ran.

"Thank you," Bailey said.

The Old Oak embraced Bailey, and in that embrace they knew *nothing* would ever harm them. They knew things the Old Oak knew. Saw things the Old Oak had seen. Things that had no name and had been forgotten before the Earth had fully formed.

Bailey smiled, and they knew the Old Oak smiled too.

Bailey walked into their house wearing the sundress. Their mother rushed over and hugged them.

"Where have you been? The school called and said th—"

Bailey hugged back. "It's okay, Mom. I'm fine."

"But I was worried sick."

"It's okay. Those bullies won't hurt me ever again."

Their mother's face scrunched up with confusion. "Who? Who hurt you? And why are you wearing this shit again? I thought we talked about that."

"No, we didn't. But we should. There's a lot of things we need to talk about if you're ready to listen."

Their mother's face went hard for a moment then softened.

"Yes. Yes, I am."

Later that night, Bailey ran their finger over a raised bit of skin on their arm. It was the same as one of the sigils they had seen on the Old Oak's trunk—a spiral with antlers. They lay in their bed listening to the wind blow outside, and for the first time ever, they could hear the Old Oak's song clearly. It sang to the other trees, telling them of things that were and things that would be.

The song would have driven most insane. But, to Bailey, it was comforting.

"The Perpetual Dance"

Gerald sat next to a campfire. The charred logs had burned out leaving nothing but glowing embers. The sun was setting behind the mountains, painting the sky in a brilliant display of oranges, reds, and yellows.

Gerald smiled. However, that smile faded from his face as a cold thought slithered into his mind.

He had no idea how he had gotten up into the mountains.

Gerald stood and spun in a slow circle. Next to the fire pit was an old green tent that was faded from sun exposure. His car was nowhere to be seen, nor was there any road. As far as he could tell, he was alone.

"Hello?"

The only answer was the caw of a nearby raven. He called out again, but this time even the bird didn't reply.

The tent wasn't his. The last time he'd been camping was over ten years ago. He didn't like the outdoors. Gerald much preferred the comforts of home, the skyscrapers cutting into the skyline, and the hustle and bustle of the city streets.

The tent's door was unzipped and flapped gently in the breeze. Inside there was a battery-operated lantern and a large manila envelope. He flipped the switch on the lantern, and it filled the inside of the tent with a bright fluorescent glow.

Gerald opened the envelope and found dozens of Polaroid photos. The pictures were of an old trail surrounded by dead pine trees. The first few were on the trail itself. The next set showed a giant pine tree in the distance. It was three times as big as any other tree in the picture and stretched high into the sky.

Something about the tree was off. It made his hand tremble, and his breathing became labored. He almost couldn't breathe at all.

As Gerald flipped through the photos, the tree got closer and closer. As it did, he noticed that something was carved on its ancient trunk. As the pictures continued to get closer to the tree, the carving became clear.

It was a simple triangle.

It was familiar, although he couldn't place where he'd seen it. Once the thought entered his head, he couldn't get rid of it, like a fine sliver stuck in your finger.

Gerald dropped the envelope and left the tent. As he exited, his vision blurred and the trees appeared to loom towards him. It was as if they wanted to snatch him up and take him away to somewhere dark and wet. He gasped and fell backward.

Gerald's vision cleared, and as it did, he was able to pull in a big lungful of air. The trees were just trees and nothing was trying to get him. However, something caught his eye.

On a nearby pine tree was a carved triangle. It was the same as in the picture, although much smaller and not the same tree.

Gerald got to his feet. He grabbed the lantern from the tent and walked over to the carved tree. It hadn't been there before. Then again, that didn't mean much. He couldn't remember how he even got to this patch of woods, so missing a small carving wasn't too far outside the realm of expectations.

The triangle wasn't much bigger than a grapefruit. It was old, as the carving was weathered and scarred. It was rough, and Gerald couldn't shake the thought that human hands had clawed it into the bark.

Deeper into the timber was blanketed in shadows. However, another triangle stood out against the darkness on a tree about twenty yards in. Further in, yet another.

Gerald stood at the tree line for a few moments before stepping into the forest. Perhaps this trail of triangles would lead him to a road.

He made his way toward the far tree that bore the carving. As he did, the temperature dropped. Gerald blamed it on the fact that the sun had finally set.

As he neared the tree, another carving appeared on the trunk of another pine further into the forest. As he followed the trees, a trail began to form beneath his feet. Deadfall pines lined either side of the trail, just like in the photos.

The fact that he was on an actual trail gave him hope. Trails led to destinations. Destinations meant possibly people and help.

He continued walking for hours.

Gerald was cold, hungry, and tired. His feet hurt with each step, and he was sure that they were covered in blisters. But what other choice did he have?

He was starting to think staying at the tent may have been a better plan, at least until morning, when in the distance, a tall pine towered above the others.

It was the tree from the picture.

Gerald's throat constricted with the sight, and once again it became difficult to breathe. He rubbed this neck and moved on.

The branches of this pine twisted outward, farther than any evergreen he'd ever encountered before. Just like in the picture, there was a carving on the trunk. Gerald already knew what it would be. However, unlike the picture, there were other things in the tree.

Bodies hanging from their necks swayed from the massive branches like macabre ornaments. They danced in the wind in a slow waltz. Gerald wanted to turn and go the other way, but his feet carried him forward. By the time he staggered up next to the massive pine, tears ran down his face and he gasped for air.

The triangle blazed with amber energy. Gerald dropped the lantern and lost himself in the light.

When the light faded, he sat next to a smoldering campfire. Inside the pit was nothing more than glowing coals and ash. The sun had descended behind the tall peaks, painting the sky with a dazzling array of colors.

He smiled as he stared at the sky, but Gerald broke into a cold sweat as a thought slithered into his mind.

He had been here before.

"THE DEEP TIMBER"

*O**h, Aspen tree, what have you seen? What do you see when you look at me?*

Utah Territory, 1884

I couldn't feel my fingers anymore, which meant starting a fire was going to be harder than shooting the ass off a fly at fifty paces. Whether or not we should even light a fire was still under some debate, as the matter of Gerald's posse and their current location was the topic on all our minds. However, freezing to death was becoming more and more likely, and the option of warmth was becoming more and more desirable.

I pulled my old bearskin coat a little tighter around my body. It used to be my dad's before me, and his dad's before him. He used to tell me that Grandpa Rick killed and skinned a grizzly that attacked him up in the north with nothing but a hunting knife. Who knows if that story was true or not, but the coat kept me from dying as we rode further up the damned mountain.

The aspens gave way to pine as we climbed up in elevation. It became colder, but at least I didn't have to have all those damn aspens staring at me. The way the knots looked like eyes sent shivers up my back like they were judging me, staring at my soul or something.

I urged my horse up to the front of the line. He gave a huff but trotted through the snow.

Old Tommy was at the lead, followed by the Rotgut twins, Colt and Walter. Trailing behind us was that Navajo friend of Tommy's named Sani. I didn't think Sani was going to make it much farther. He'd taken a bullet in the leg a few days back as we made dust out of Evanston. That wound had started to sour, and none of his Navajo tricks were making a difference.

Old Tommy had his hat pulled low and was smoking his pipe. He cast me an angry look as I neared.

"Think it's smart lighting that pipe of yours? I bet they can smell it over in the next canyon."

He grunted and shrugged his shoulders. "I reckon Gerald and his boys are just as cold and lost as we are up in this timber. If I'm going to freeze to death, might as well do so with a nice warm pipe full of tobacco."

Tommy wasn't wrong. We'd gotten turned around half a dozen times already. The lodgepoles made it hard to navigate, and if it hadn't been for Sani, I'm sure we'd have been chewing up dirt going in circles. However, Sani wasn't saying much anymore, not that the man was a chatterbox to begin with. His skin was looking mighty pale, and he had that stare I'd seen plenty of times before. It was the look you'd get when Death was on your tail.

"We should probably set up camp soon."

Tommy nodded. "Sure. Let's get it done before the sun sets."

We picked a spot near the mouth of a small draw. A little creek cut through the snow and provided a bit of background noise. While it covered our sounds, it made it difficult to hear anyone coming.

Tommy strode up to me, still puffing on that pipe. I didn't like the look in his eye. His twisted mind was churning.

"Best if you take an extra blanket and go up the hill a bit, be our lookout for the night."

I took my hat off and shook some of the snow off the brim. "Send one of the Rotgut twins. Hell, they'd probably think it's some grand bandit adventure!"

Ever since Tommy brought them into the fold, they'd gone on and on about living the good life, free from the law. I think they actually believed that being an outlaw meant wandering from town to town, meeting a different señorita each night, and drinking their fill of cheap whiskey. They were sorely disappointed when it meant staying on the outskirts of most places so as to not get noticed and trying not to get sick from dirty water.

"I need someone with their wits about them tonight. Sani's about to keel over, and those two morons have already started into the spirits."

The Rotgut twins were singing a song about some scantily dressed whore or something and giggling up a storm. I let out a sigh as it was going to be a cold night.

"Now if you see something, sneak on back and let us know. If you can't get back in time..."

I held up a hand to stop him. "I know, I know, shoot once in the air."

"Good man. Now head on up there. I'll try and spell you in a while."

While it was kind of him to say, it was a lie. Tommy would be snoring before too long, and I would on my own.

I made my way up the hill. It wasn't too far, but it was steep, and before too long I was huffing and puffing. The cool air burned my lungs and put a feather in the back of my throat. I didn't want to be drenched in sweat and die frozen under a pine tree, so I took a moment to rest about halfway up. The Rotguts' song floated up from below, and I shook my head. Those bastards would be the death of us if they didn't keep it down. Hopefully, Tommy was right, and Gerald's gang was just as lost as we were. But my granddaddy always said hope was fool's gold, nice but worthless.

I was about to start my ascent again when the snap of a tree from above echoed through the draw.

I ducked down and drew my pistol.

It was loud enough it even got the Rotgut twins' attention and their song trailed off with the wind.

I glanced back down to camp. Tommy and the others were all staring up at me, their weapons drawn. After a moment, Tommy shooed me onward with a wave of his hand.

I crawled up the hillside slow and easy. I didn't want to be gasping or coughing like a lunger when I got to the top. I needed my wits about me and my aim to be true. I was almost at the crest when another branch snapped, this time closer.

I stopped and listened.

My heartbeat drummed in my ears, accompanied by heavy breaths. I couldn't keep the slight shake from my hand as I took those final few steps, unsure of what lay in wait for me up above. My brain tried to say it was nothing. Just old branches givin' up the fight against the weight of the snow. Hell, I'd even take Gerald and his posse. Yet my gut screamed at me, saying it was something worse than hired guns or weather-laden sticks. My gut told me to run and never stop until these damned mountains were long behind me.

I inched my way to the top and peeked over.

There was nobody there. Just trees and more snow. A couple of ravens sat on a branch of a tall pine and stared at me like I was some fool sent for their amusement. Perhaps I was.

I walked around where I thought the sound may have come from and found the source.

A dead pine had fallen over. A widowmaker.

After a moment, I walked back to the edge and waved to Tommy and the gang. The Rotgut twins started singing and laughing like nothing had ever happened. Tommy nodded and emptied his pipe into the snow. Sani stared up at me with wide eyes. Even from the distance, I could see the fear.

I set myself up in a spot far away from the fallen tree. It was stupid, but I didn't want to be anywhere near that thing when the sun decided to set. I bundled up with my blankets, but as soon as I stopped moving, the chill set in. I debated whether or not I should light a fire. It would give away my position, but on the other hand, I wouldn't be any good as a lookout if I died from the cold.

The dead see things. They can see you.

I didn't know where those words had come from. I hadn't heard anything like that before. It had come from nowhere, the idea forming in my head and burrowing deep. Perhaps I overheard Sani talking beside a campfire one night. That had to be it. He was always rambling about spiritual nonsense when he thought nobody was listening.

I rubbed my forehead. A small ache had started just behind my eye. I took a drink from my waterskin. The water was cold just like everything else, but it soothed my parched throat. The waterskin was almost empty, and I'd have to remember to fill it in the morning before we broke camp and left.

Getting the fire going took some time, but it was worth it. The warmth from the flames brought my fingers back from the brink and staved off the chill enough to keep me alive.

The Rotgut twins started singing louder. Their voices rode the wind and swept past my ears with a slight warble. Generally in tune, it was easy to mistake the singing of the Rotgut Twins as just one person; however, this song was disjointed, broken. Tommy must have got after the two, because the singing stopped just as quick as it had come, leaving nothing but silence in its wake.

Even with the biting cold nipping at my nose and seeping into my legs, it was hard to keep my eyes open. Being on the run for the past couple of days had drained me. I kept the fire going, but the rhythmic dance of the flames was beckoning me beyond the Wall of the Sleep. At one point I nodded off only to jolt awake moments later.

The crunch of a boot in the snow did the trick. I scrambled to my feet and drew my pistol.

"Who's there?"

I pulled the hammer back and pointed it into the darkness.

"If I had wanted to kill you, you'd be dead already."

Sani stepped from the shadows and into the firelight. I let out a sigh and holstered my weapon.

"Good god, don't you know it's dangerous to go slinking about?"

Sani smiled, though it was strained.

"I find it's equally as dangerous to let folks know I'm there."

I shrugged my shoulders. "Fair enough." I motioned him to the fire.

"I brought coffee."

"Well, why didn't you say so? I could hug you!"

Sani shuffled closer and sat on the ground with a groan. I dug my tin cup from my satchel and held it out so he could pour me some coffee from the pot he'd carried with him. At that moment, Sani was a godsend, an angel sent from the heavens to deliver ambrosia upon the faithful. Except, he wasn't an angel, I wasn't faithful, and the coffee, while hot, wasn't anywhere close to the food of the gods.

"How's the wound?"

"How do you think?"

I nodded. "Maybe we can get you to a doc or something in Ashley?"

"That's what I like about you, you keep hold of hope like it is your last gold nugget."

I wasn't sure how to take that, as I had a problem holding on to money. You could ask my wife about that. One of the reasons she took the girls and went back East to her parents' house. I'm sure her parents gave her an earful about how they knew it would turn out that way and she was better off without me.

I was sure she'd take me back if I could get enough money to keep us comfortable. Old Tommy kept talking about a plan to rob the payroll and making it big. It sounded nice, but I couldn't help but wonder how my little girls were doing. Their laughs were worth more than silver or gold.

"This will all be over soon."

Sani must have seen the darkness on my face. I took a sip of coffee and let the warm liquid roll down my throat.

"I hope so. Hey, what's your deal anyway? Why are you riding with Tommy?"

Sani had been with Tommy since before I joined up. Tommy treated the man with respect and deferred to his wisdom in many situations. Once I saw Tommy knock the teeth out of a cowpoke who made an offhand remark about Sani's heritage. I didn't care much where a person was from—Navajo, Apache, Mexican. Hell, as long as they didn't try to kill me and pulled their weight, people were fine by me.

"I am here because of my brother."

It was Sani's turn to wear a dark mask. He lowered his head and stared at the flames of my small fire.

"I'm not following. Where's your brother?"

Sani placed the coffee pot near the fire and folded his arms into his blanket.

"He died four years ago. We were running from a posse, much like today. Only it was him who took a bullet in the stomach."

"I'm sorry."

"I told him it was foolish to follow the path of greed. Nothing good would come of it. He would not be swayed by my words, nor the words of our mother. So I followed him. To protect him. I failed. Now I ride with Tommy because I have nowhere else to go."

I didn't know what to say, so I said nothing. A few moments later, the Rotguts started singing again. I reckon the whiskey was starting to settle in their blood and it made them anxious.

Sani closed his eyes. "We must not attract attention."

"Because of Gerald's posse?"

"Because there is something in this woods that wants us." Sani stood with a groan. "We should not have wandered from the trail. My people tell stories of foolish boys who wandered too far into the timber. The trees, they watch and wait."

He winced at his first step and wandered back down the trail. He had left me the coffee, which was kind. Yet, I couldn't help but think of things other than coffee.

There was a small stain of blood in the snow where Sani had been sitting.

The Rotgut twins finally stopped their singing. Hopefully, Tommy knocked some sense into those two. About an hour later, I had burned through the pot of coffee and it had started to work its dark magic on me. I got up, careful to keep my blanket around my body, although it wasn't doing much good with the biting cold. I shuffled off a few feet and answered the call of nature.

There was a crunch of feet in the snow. I turned and drew my pistol, still hanging free in the wind. It was cold, but I had other things to deal with. Standing in the dark was a tall figure. The firelight hit the person's eyes just right and they flashed, almost like a cougar or something. It happened so quick, I couldn't focus on it.

Whoever it was had wild hair sticking out in all directions and smelled awful. Like shit and sweat. It had to be one of the Rotguts.

"What you doing up here? Did Tommy send you up?"

No answer. He just stood there and stared at me. I took a moment to do up my pants and wrap the blanket around me again.

"Well, what is it? You drunk? You can't sit up here on watch and be blasted out of your skull. Go back down there and get some rest."

Still, he stood there. I was about to walk over and push whichever one of those damned twins it was back down the hillside when he turned and walked away. As he did, his joints made sounds like old wood groaning or the grind of bone on bone.

I went back to my fire and sat back down. I kept my gun out resting on my leg. There were more sounds coming from the darkness. Like the trees moving. Not just swaying in the wind, as the wind wasn't blowing. But like they were getting up and walking around.

I dreamt I was surrounded by old trees and they were all staring down at my corpse. They whispered things. Things I couldn't hear. Those creaks and groans of branch and bone filled the sky and soon I couldn't hear anything at all. Anything but the screams of Colt cutting up the hillside.

It was the screams that woke me.

My face flushed with heat when I realized I'd fallen asleep on watch. If Old Tommy found out, I was a dead man.

I ran over to the hillside and looked down at the camp. Colt was pacing around and running a hand through that patch of ginger mess he called hair. He was yelling about something. Something about his brother missing.

I ran down the hill and almost tripped on an exposed root. Sani was sitting on a large boulder. He had a pained expression on his face and nodded as I walked by.

"What's going on?" It was hard to get the words out. Being so high up in the mountains was taking a toll on my lungs.

Old Tommy shot me a look that sent chills up my back even in the morning cold. Colt turned my way with a crazy look in his eye. A trail of dried drool ran down his chin coupled with fresh tears that had chiseled a path down his grimy cheeks. He stumbled over to me, still drunk, and grabbed my shoulders.

"You! You were on watch! What happened to him?"

I looked around and it dawned me.

"Where's Walter?"

Colt spun around in a circle and rubbed the back of his neck. His shoulder popped.

Those creaks and groans of branch and bone...

"That's what I was asking you!"

Old Tommy stepped up and put an arm around Colt's shoulder.

"It's okay. I'm sure he just wandered off in a drunken stupor. We'll find him. Hell, in this snow it will be easy to follow his tracks."

Tracks. It had to have been Walter standing outside of my campfire last night.

"Hold on, I think he came up last night. I thought he wandered back down to camp!"

I took off running back up the hill. At one point I was crawling on all fours it was so steep. My lungs burned. I should have taken my time, but if I could find the tracks perhaps I could redeem myself for falling asleep. They didn't know I passed out, but I knew, and that was enough.

It wasn't the first time I'd failed at my responsibilities.

I missed my girls.

I got to the top and almost fell over as the world spun. I sucked in big ol' gulps of air until I could finally breathe then hurried over to where I had camped. The pot of coffee sat next to a pile of ashes. After a quick search, I found my tracks and patch of yellow snow, and it wasn't too hard to find the other tracks. I wished I hadn't though.

The tracks showed bare feet with spots of blood. Whoever made the tracks had an irregular stride, steps sometimes close together, other times longer than a normal person should have been able to step. I followed them away from my site to a patch of thick timber. Lodgepole pines stretched up into the sky like rows upon rows of jagged teeth.

The footprints stopped at the edge of the trees and disappeared. I looked all around but couldn't find them again. The hairs on the back of my neck stood up, and the chirping birds went silent. Some of the trees swayed lazily with the breeze. There was a low moan of wood as a pine moved against another.

Deep in the woods, something cracked like thunder.

"Well, did you find him?"

I jumped at the voice and spun around. Old Tommy let out a chuckle and held his hands up.

"Just me."

"Good lord, Tommy! Make some noise next time."

A wave of dizziness hit me. I leaned up against one of the trees to steady myself. There was something sticky on the tree and it was warm and made me want to throw up. I pulled my hand away expecting sap, but it was some sort of black goop. I dropped to my knee and grabbed a handful of snow to wash it away. It left a black stain on my palm and made my hand tingle.

"Well?"

I looked up at Tommy. "Well, what?"

"Did you find him?"

"No, followed these tracks to the tree line," I said pointing behind me.

Tommy turned and looked.

"What tracks?"

I growled a bit and stood. "These tracks! Are you blind?"

I turned to show him but the tracks were gone. Never there.

"What in the hell?!"

Tommy placed a hand on my shoulder. He had a genuine look of concern in his eye.

"It was... never mind. Look, I think he went in there."

In with the timber, in the with the bones, creaking and groaning, listen to the moans.

I rubbed at my forehead. "Did you hear that?"

"Hear what?"

"Nothing," I said.

"Well, if you think he went that way, then that's good enough for me. More than likely that damned fool wandered off drunk last night and is frozen to death somewhere. Take Colt and go look for him."

I shook my head. No way I was taking that crazy drunk ass fool.

"I'll go alone, it will be quicker and quieter."

Tommy's eyes went dark for a moment. "I don't think I stuttered. Take Colt. Otherwise, he'll be yelling like a madman all through these woods. Be back before midday whether you find Walter or not. We're moving then."

I sighed. I knew from experience that I wouldn't win the argument and trying to do so would only make Tommy angry. When he got angry it was like stepping into a pit of vipers. You could possibly make it out unscathed, but more than likely you were going to get bit and probably die.

"Fine. Send him up. I'm not crawling up and down that hillside anymore."

"Good boy."

Heat flashed in my cheeks. I hated it when he called me a good boy like I was a damn dog or something. I watched him walk away and contemplated putting a bullet in his back. My hand was already on my gun when I realized what I was doing. I let out a blast of breath that I'd been holding in. I couldn't figure out where that thought had come from, it wasn't like me. The world spun, and I puked up coffee. It was black like the goop on the tree.

It wasn't too much longer before Colt's mumbling and bellows echoed up the hill to my ears. It was going to be a long trek through the woods. I wiped my face and waited for Colt.

We made our way through the trees. At first, Colt called out for Walter, and it took me threatening to cave in his skull for him to stop.

"We'll bring down Gerald and his posse for sure if you keep hollerin' like that!"

"We need to find Walter!"

I rubbed my forehead. A giant pain was brewing, and I wanted to get somewhere warm and sleep for a week. Instead, I was stuck in the timber with this idiot.

"We'll find him, but we need to do it quieter, or else it won't matter if we find him or not."

Colt looked at me with crazy eyes. "It don't matter if we die. We need to find him."

I couldn't respond to that kind of crazy. There wasn't anything anyone could say. So I stayed quiet.

As long as I kept moving, I stayed warm enough. I kept that wool blanket wrapped around me, but whenever we'd stop to rest or to listen, that biting cold slithered into my bones. It was during one of those stops that the cawing of crows broke through the silence. It was more than just chattering birds or warning caws. They were announcing a feast.

Something was dead.

"Come on," I said.

We made our way through the trees, but they grew closer and closer together, and there was a lot of deadfall on the ground. I felt like I wasn't supposed to go any further, but I wasn't about to let some fallen trees tell me what to do. I always did what I wanted.

That's why we can't stay with you anymore. I'm taking the girls.

I shook my head to clear the voices and pressed forward. The trees tried like hell to keep us out, but we had cold determination on our side. We scrambled across a large dead pine and broke through to a clearing. It wasn't very large. Hell, I could have probably thrown a tomahawk from one tree line to the other, and I wasn't even that good at it. But it wasn't the open meadow that held my attention, no, it was the blood in the snow.

There was tons of it, spread all over hell and back. And the smell, dear lord, the smell was thick with the iron-like scent of blood. It had to be Gerald's posse. There was a campfire, still smoking, with bedrolls strewn about. Whatever happened had happened while they slept.

I drew my pistol and moved to get a closer look. Colt followed close behind, his gun in hand as well.

"What the hell happened here?" Colt asked.

"I don't know. Where is everyone?"

With all the blood, there had to be a body somewhere. I searched around, poking my head into a lone tent that had been set up near the trees. The side was ripped. Inside, the smell of death and shit hit me like a punch to the gut, and I about threw up.

There wasn't a body, but there was a pile of entrails in the corner.

I staggered out, coughing and covering my face.

"Don't," I said as Colt wandered over to the tent. "You don't need to see that."

He glared at me and went on ahead like a stubborn mule. A second later he fell out of the tent with a wail.

"Jesus! Jesus damned Christ! What is this?"

"I don't know. Come on though, that fire was going not too long ago, let's see if we can find where they went."

I walked around looking for tracks. With the snow, it wasn't hard to find them. It looked like they had run off through the woods.

I motioned for Colt and set off after them. Not sure why really. It wasn't like it would do us any good if we found the posse. Yet, there was something deep down inside that needed to know. Besides, they could have Walter.

At the edge of the meadow, we found more tracks, different than the others. They were also barefoot, but there were a lot of them, at least a dozen sets. They circled the meadow, sticking to the tree line, and had that odd gait similar to the tracks where I had set up watch. We found their horses. They were all dead, lined up and missing their heads.

Their heads hadn't been cut off; something had ripped them off. Jagged bits of flesh and bone littered the ground. This time, I did throw up.

Colt stared at the horses with a wide-eyed look of someone who had lost their last ounce of sanity. A bit of drool ran down from the corner of his mouth, and his hands were shaking.

"Come on, let's go," I said.

Colt didn't respond, so I just grabbed his arm and pulled him with me. We needed to find his brother and get back to camp before Old Tommy decided we weren't worth the trouble to stick around anymore.

We followed the posse's tracks further into the woods. Whatever got them moving had lit a fire under their feet, for Gerald's boys had run from camp and hadn't stopped.

Colt followed along staring off at nothing. I'd seen that look before. Some of the men who had fought in the war had that same look sometimes.

There was a loud crack and boom as if a tree had fallen nearby. Then another. And another! It was getting closer.

I did what any sane man would have—I ran. Thankfully, Colt followed close behind. I ran as fast as I could and had to dodge trees and rocks with almost every step.

The thing followed, crashing through the forest like a stampede of angry bison. I didn't look back. I couldn't. To do so would have broken me, for if I saw whatever it was that came for us, I knew I'd be a goner.

I shouldered through some pines and found myself face to face with a rock wall. A breath later, Colt stumbled beside me. We were both gasping for air, sweat pouring down our faces. If the thing didn't kill us, the cold air would.

"What now?" Colt asked.

I pointed up and holstered my pistol. "We climb."

The thing was getting closer, but I scrambled up the rock wall and somehow didn't slip and fall to my death. I could picture it in my mind's eye, falling and snapping my legs, laying there in the snow as the thing slowly devoured me.

Those creaks and groans of branch and bone...

Somehow, I made it to the top and instantly wished I hadn't.

Sitting in the snow were the horses' heads. Right next to them were the heads of Gerald and his posse. Their eyes had been ripped out along with the skin around their mouth, giving them all horrible grins that would have sent shivers up Death's spine.

Colt made it up right after me. He stopped before he crawled up all the way and stared at all the heads. Tears ran down his cheeks and he kept mumbling something. I couldn't quite hear what it was but did catch a word or two.

"...the eyes in the aspens..."

"What did you say?"

He stopped speaking and looked at me.

"Tell Old Tommy I'm sorry."

Before I could say anything else he let go and fell off the rock wall. He fell to the earth with a sick thud and a crack.

"No! God damn it!"

Colt looked up at me with blood coming from his nose and mouth. He opened his mouth to say something but only let out a wet gurgle. He coughed, sending flecks of bloody spittle flying in all directions.

Before I could even start to crawl back down, something grabbed him by the shoulder and dragged him into the trees. My heart froze and my stomach dropped. There was a crack...

Those creaks and groans of branch and bone...

...and then a tear. A moment later, Colt's head came rolling out into the clearing.

I ran.

I'm not sure how I found my way back to camp or how I didn't freeze to death, but when I arrived, I couldn't feel my hands or feet anymore. Sani was by a campfire that was burning tall and hot. I stumbled over towards it and fell at his feet. I don't know what happened next, as everything went black.

When I woke, I was back home lying in my old, rickety bed I had fashioned from a cedar. One good shake and the thing was going to fall apart. I kept meaning to fix it, or make a new one, a better one, but never got around to it. I was covered in sweat and felt hot, so I kicked off the blankets. The cool air touched my skin, and I lay in the bed staring at the old timber that held our roof up.

There were giggles from the next room followed by the angry whispers of my wife telling the girls to keep quiet, lest they wanted to wake me. I smiled, couldn't help it.

I sat up and shuffled over to the doorway. My hips and shoulders hurt something fierce, and my head felt like it was going to bust open at any moment. I had to steady myself before I fell over.

"Oh look, you woke up your father. He's going to be mighty angry with you."

I walked over to the table and sat in the chair. "It's okay, honey, I was already awake."

The girls giggled again and ran over to me. They were like two little angels with hair the color of a wheat field and eyes bluer than a cornflower. I scooped them up into a big hug and held them tight. They groaned and tried to get away, but I didn't want to let them go. I took in a deep breath and my heart skipped a beat.

They smelled like dead leaves and rotting meat.

I dropped them to the ground and they snapped like dried twigs. They continued to giggle. My wife ambled up behind me, lumbering like some great beast.

"He's going to be mighty angry with you."

Her voice was dry and raspy. She placed a hand on my shoulder, and it was rough and skeletal.

I didn't want to turn around, but she placed another hand on the other shoulder and spun me around with profound strength.

I screamed and screamed until my throat was raw. I screamed until someone shook me so hard my teeth rattled.

"Wake up. It is a dream."

It was Sani's voice. I was next to the fire wrapped in three blankets. I scrambled backward and shed the blankets like a snakeskin.

"Where am I? What's going on?"

Sani placed another log on the fire and looked at me. His eyes were bloodshot, and his skin was almost as white as the snow.

"You are back at camp."

I looked around; there wasn't anyone else. I remembered Walter had run off and Colt had...Colt was gone.

"Old Tommy?"

Sani shook his head. "Left before mid-day."

"Damn it."

"He said he was not going to die out here waiting for you to get back."

It sounded like Tommy. "Why didn't you go with him?"

Sani looked at me and gave me a pained smile. "I'm already dead. I'm waiting for my spirit to realize it."

"Nonsense. Let's get the hell out of here. I have no idea where Walter went, but Colt's dead. So is the posse."

"I'm not going anywhere."

Well, I sure as shit wasn't going to stick around and freeze to death. I got up and shuffled over to my horse. At least Tommy had the decency to leave it behind, though I surmised it was more for speed than doing me any favors.

I got into the saddle and my back screamed at me to stop. I needed a bottle of whiskey and a week's worth of sleep. I looked over to Sani and found him staring back at me.

"What's out there?" I asked.

"Our sins coming for us. We are bad men. Our days of robbing and fighting could not last forever."

"That doesn't make a lick of sense," I said.

"It doesn't have to."

I wanted to be with my family. Not up here freezing to death. I gave a nod to Sani who nodded back.

It was going to be the last time I ever saw him, I knew that much. With that, I kicked my horse and headed down the trail. I needed to get off this cursed mountain and into a warm saloon soon, or I was going to be as dead as everyone else.

Old Tommy's tracks were easy to follow in the snow. It wasn't the usual route to Ashley, but perhaps he was still trying to avoid the posse. Tommy had no idea that the posse wasn't a threat anymore. I didn't want to be alone, so I kicked my horse into a run and hoped I could catch up.

His tracks wound up a hillside and back down again. A large pond that was starting to ice over came into view. Way on the other side, two figures stepped out from the trees. One waved at me with jerky movements. The other didn't have a head.

It was the Rotgut twins.

I looked away and went faster. I didn't look back, afraid of what I might see, but the weight of the forest watching me was heavier than a wet wool blanket. The wind rushed past my ears and bit the skin on my face, but I didn't dare slow down. If I did, they would catch me.

"Dadda?"

The voice came out of nowhere, and my horse whinnied and reared back, dumping me into the snow. Before I could get up and grab the reins, it took off screaming and wide-eyed.

"Damn it! Get back here!"

It was hopeless though. That horse was halfway to Fort Bridger by now. I sat there in the snow, not sure what to do next.

There was a snap of a branch and the woods fell silent. I spun around. There, at the edge of the pines, was a group of aspen trees. Had they been there before? I didn't notice any aspens when I had ridden by, just pines.

The hair on the back of my neck stood, and a shiver ran through my body. I stood and followed Tommy's trail. Thankfully, it led away from those trees, as the eye-like knots watched my every movement. Hungry, as if I were a prize.

As I crunched through frost-encrusted snow, there was another sound. At first, I thought it was just me walking, but I would stop and it continued. A low creak and snap, as wood moved.

I spun around to find the aspen trees still there, but they had changed location. They were spread out. Not just in a clump together.

I picked up the pace and started to run. As I did, the Rotgut Twins started singing from the timber. Their song rose into the air and wavered. It was the same song they sang the night before, but it lacked joy. Instead, it was rushed, like they were forced to sing it faster than normal. It picked up tempo, and the Rotgut Twins sang louder.

I moved as fast as I could, and Tommy's trail started to go down a hill. The pines gave way to more and more aspen the further down I went.

They were all watching me, and I swore I could hear them breathing, laughing, and mocking me as I went. Then came a thunderous crack that echoed through the draw and ripped through my ears. I couldn't help but let out a cry and drop to my knees. There were creaks and groans from behind me. I didn't want to look. I wanted to keep going and find Tommy. But I couldn't help it.

All of the aspens were bent toward me, their branches pointing at me like accusing fingers. A shadow of movement caught my eye, and I slowly turned my head. Standing there in the trees was Walter. His eyes were gone, and the pits looked like the knots in the trees. His grin was wide, much wider than it should have been. He pointed at me and opened his mouth.

The Rotgut's song came from deep inside him as his mouth stayed open and unmoving.

Down near the aspen trees
Feel the fear, hear the screams
Down near the aspen trees
What have you seen
What do you see when you look at me
Down near the aspen trees

With those creaks and groans of branch and bone
We'll grind your bones to dust and stone

Walter turned his head until he was looking right at me. He moved his arm and pointed a finger, and when he did it sounded like trees moaning in the wind. His mouth was still open, but the song had stopped. What came out of his mouth next was more horrifying than anything else.

You're never here anymore. I just don't feel safe. I'm taking the girls with me and going back home.

My wife's voice floated from deep inside Walter's body and got louder and louder until it came from every direction. I covered my ears and dropped to my knees.

"This ain't real! You ain't real!"

I screamed until my voice was shredded and broken.

When I opened my eyes, there were aspens all around me, staring at me with their black and dead eyes.

I came to, walking down the trail. I don't know how long I had been walking, but the sun was setting. I was shivering something fierce and couldn't feel my feet anymore. My legs were stiff. I wanted to tear my boots off and look, but I was afraid of what I'd find.

I was afraid they would be wood.

I stumbled down the path, catching glimpses of things moving in the trees—eyes that caught the setting sunlight just right and glowed, a clawed hand caressing a tree trunk. And the whispers, dear god the whispers. They came from the timber and told me things I never wanted to hear. Things I dare not repeat.

The trail became steep, and I slipped in the snow. I hit a rock with my hip on the way down and cried out as fire burned down my leg and up my back. I rolled to the bottom and just lay there for a moment wishing I was dead.

The dead see things. They can see you.

There was another sound nearby, the crack and pop of a fire and the huff and shuffle of a horse. The pleasant aroma of coffee wafted into my nose, and for a moment I thought perhaps I *had* died and this was heaven. But the pain in my back and the cold seeping into my body argued otherwise.

Besides, I had a feeling I wasn't destined for heaven.

I rolled to my stomach and pushed myself up to my knees. When I stood, the pain in my hip came alive like someone had poked me with a branding iron. I wobbled to a tree and leaned against it for support.

It moved when I touched it, slithered like a bark-covered snake.

I hobbled to the fire. Old Tommy sat next to it warming up his hands.

"You made it. I always knew you would."

"What the hell is going on?" I asked.

Old Tommy poured a cup of coffee and handed it to me. I took it and just held my hands around the cup for warmth. My fingers were red and blistered.

"Seems like we've gotten trapped here. Whatever lives in these woods doesn't want us to leave. I tried every trail I knew but kept ending up here," he said.

"But why? Why is it happening?"

Old Tommy sighed and poured himself a cup of coffee.

"My grandpappy used to tell me stories of the deep timber. How if you went waltzin' in them woods and brought a sour heart that sometimes it would attract the attention of them trees and those dark things that lived in them. He said, always stay on the trails and try and keep that bitterness in the foothills, for the timber was a place a violent man could meet a violent end."

He took his pipe out and lit it, and when the match flared to life, the firelight exposed his eyes. They were tree knots, twisted and black.

Tommy looked at me and smiled. His skin cracked around his lips and on his cheeks.

I turned to run and was surrounded by trees. They moved in on me, so thick I couldn't see through them.

I let out a yell and jumped on Tommy's horse. We beat hell out of that meadow. The trees scratched at my face and grabbed my clothes. Their bony fingers dug into skin and burrowed as deep as they could as I raced past, but I didn't care. Blood ran freely into my eyes, and I could barely see.

I never looked back, and I pushed that horse until it died on that mountainside. Once it fell, I got up and ran. I ran as far as I could until up was down and left was right.

They say when I stumbled into the streets of Ashley I was covered in mud and blood and had a crazed look in my eye. They say it took four men to hold me down so the doc could fix me up.

But I don't remember any of it. All I remember is the trees. Those damned trees everywhere, looking at me.

The trees were one of the reasons why I was so nervous to go back east to find my family. There were so many trees out that way. Perhaps, once I found them, we could go somewhere where there weren't any trees.

I held the train ticket in my hand, a small thing, but it was heavier than a sack of gold nuggets. Just looking at the damned thing got my heart running wild.

"Coming home," I said, barely more than a whisper.

The train rumbled toward the station spewing black smoke and screaming like a hellhound. It lumbered to a stop in front of me, and for a few moments all I could do was stare at it. This damned thing would take me back to my girls and that was that. I was done running and gunning. I'd take a job cutting down trees or moving cattle, anything to keep them in my life. As soon as I could, I boarded the train and found a seat.

I let out a sigh and sank into the cushioned bench. I closed my eyes and just let everything go. The sounds of folks boarding the train and engaging in idle chatter filled my head.

But there was something else. A sound that sort of tip-toed through the rest of the noise. Like branches swaying in a breeze behind me.

My eyes shot open, and I spun around in my chair. A woman wearing a blue dress recoiled in her seat and looked at me with wide, fright-filled eyes.

I searched but couldn't find anything out of the ordinary.

"Sorry, ma'am."

She shot me an icy look and moved to another seat, muttering about the train letting on certain types of people or some sort of nonsense. I faced forward and rubbed at my temples. Since my ordeal in the woods, the smallest thing set me on edge. I closed my eyes and rested my head against the window.

When I woke, the train was moving and we were somewhere in the plains. Rolling hills covered with grass filled the view as far as the eye could see. The wind blew and the grass gave its best impression of the ocean. Best of all, there were no trees.

My neck ached from sleeping in an odd position for too long. It was stiff and cracked when I moved it. I rubbed at the back of my neck with my hand and stopped when my fingers brushed across something hard. It was like a scab but harder.

I picked at it, and pain jumped through my whole body. Pain or not, I was damned curious now. I gritted my teeth and grabbed on to a bit of the hard substance and pulled. Fire ran down my neck, and my stomach lurched. I let out a grunt of pain but pulled some more. Whatever it was, was attached and pulled my skin along with it, tearing a bit, and I yanked harder. With one final pull, it tore free, taking a strip of flesh along as a prize.

My hands were shaking as I brought the hard piece around to take a look. Sweat poured down my face and my breathing was haggard. I held a bloody strip of skin in my fingers. I flipped it over and immediately threw it on the floor.

It was a piece of bark.

Someone started humming a tune behind me, the same tune the Rotguts had sung back in the timber. I whirled and searched the faces of the passengers, looking for Colt or Walter. There he was. He sat at the very back with his hat brim pulled so low it hid his face. But nothing could hide that mess of hair that was redder than a young boy's face visiting a brothel for the first time.

I stood and drew my pistol. The nearby passengers gasped and shrank away from me like I was a monster. There were screams and guffaws as I passed by. One cowpoke stood up thinking he was going to be a hero or something.

"Now put that gun away like a good boy before anyone gets hurt."

I turned my attention to the man and sneered. "This ain't any of your business, now get out of the way!"

"Want to think twice about that?" He pulled his jacket to the side and exposed a tin star on his vest. His other hand rested on the ivory-handled grip of his pistol holstered on his hip.

My mind raced. I couldn't afford to make a scene, not when I was so close to getting back to my family. But on the other hand, *he* was back there waiting. I glanced at the back of the train, but the man was gone. I looked everywhere but couldn't find him.

"Okay, okay. Sorry about that. Just had a bit to drink and a bad dream."

I put my pistol away and put my hands in the air.

"You just sit down, be quiet, and don't make any more fuss, and we'll forget this ever happened. Got it?"

I wanted to bash the lawman's skull in and crack his bones like twigs.

I rubbed at my head.

"Of course, Marshal. Of course."

I went and sat back in my seat. A few of the nearby passengers got up and moved away from me. Couldn't blame them one bit.

The rest of the train ride passed without event. I spent most of the time trying to sleep and avoid the marshal. I kept an eye out for the red-haired stranger, but I couldn't find him again.

After a long journey, the train finally stopped at my destination. I stepped off onto the platform and took a deep breath. The air here was different, hard to explain. I much preferred the mountains, or I should say, I used to prefer the mountains. But in those ancient peaks was where the timber grew thick. Perhaps it would be better for a change of pace, and I knew it would be better with my wife and girls.

The Marshal walked off the train and shot me a look. He'd been eyeing me the whole train ride, and I figured he might have half an idea on who I was. I was wanted in a couple of the territories.

He started to walk towards me. I pulled my hat low and walked away from him and into the biggest crowd I could find. I pushed through the people and slipped into a nearby alley. The alley smelled of piss, and the muffled, off-key tune from a saloon piano came through a nearby wall.

The sun crept through the buildings in such a way that the Marshal's shadow splayed across one of the buildings. It grew bigger as he neared. I ducked behind a stack of boxes and drew my gun. I didn't want to kill the man, but I didn't go through hell and come all this way just to end up in jail.

The shadow stopped as the Marshal rounded the corner. I wanted to peek over the boxes and see if it really was him or just some passerby, but I didn't want to give away my position.

He started to come closer, moving slowly. I pulled the hammer back on my gun and winced as it clicked into place, sure the Marshal heard it.

He moved even closer. When he stepped, his joints creaked.

Those creaks and groans of branch and bone...

That humming started again. The same humming from the train.

The shadow started to run towards me. It moved in a jerky motion like it was a scarecrow that had come to life.

The creaks and cracks got louder as it closed the distance. I scrambled backward but couldn't quite get any traction in the dirt.

Just as it was almost upon me, it stopped. The boxes obscured most of it from view, but the top of its hat let me know it was standing there. Then, it spoke.

"With those creaks and groans of branch and bone, we'll grind your bones to dust and stone."

Its voice... It was deep and didn't sound like anything a human being should have sounded like. It was like the woods moving and the bugs buzzing. It was like a mountain lion screaming. It was the wind ripping the flesh from bone.

A strong gust of wind blew through the alley. It kicked up dust that got in my eyes, and I had to snap them shut or go blind. I threw my hand up to protect my face, but just as fast as the gust had come, it was gone. I wiped my eyes clear and the man was gone.

I stood and pointed my gun down the alley. My hand was shaking so bad, I was afraid I was going to send a round through the saloon wall on accident. I couldn't find the stranger. The only thing left was a few aspen leaves sitting in a pile behind the boxes.

I found my way to the house easily enough. Her father ran a sawmill and had made a name for himself. He owned a large estate outside of town. I walked up the steps to the front door and hesitated before I knocked.

I caught a glimpse of myself in the window and lamented my current state. My eyes were bloodshot and sunken with exhaustion. I was covered in dirt and dust, and there were tears in my shirt from when...

I didn't want to think about it. I found my grit and knocked on the door. A moment later it opened, and I found myself face to face with her father.

He was a tall man, thin to the point of being skeletal. He sported a bushy mustache that was the color ash and hung off his face and below his chin. His eyes narrowed when he saw me.

He opened his mouth, about to spit some curses my way I was sure. I put my hand up to stop him.

"I don't want to fight. I came back because I know I made some mistakes, and I want to make amends. I just want to be with my family now. I want to see my girls."

He looked at me for a moment before spitting on the ground. He wiped his mouth with a kerchief and spun on his heel. I halfway expected him to slam the door in my face and that would be it, but he took a few steps down the hall and stopped. When he noticed that I was still standing in the doorway, he motioned for me to follow him.

My heart lifted, and I bounded into the house after him. He led me through the main room, past the kitchen where his staff was preparing dinner. I didn't realize how hungry I was until that wonderful scent of venison stew hit my nose. My stomach growled, and I had to stop myself from grabbing a slice of cheese off the counter as we passed by. I was here to make a good impression, and I'd be damned if a little thing like hunger was going to ruin it any further.

He led me to the back and opened the door.

"Well, go on then," he said. His voice was gruff.

I wasn't too sure what was going on or why he wanted me to go out into the back yard. Then I heard it—the laughter of my little girls.

I stepped out of the house and couldn't stop the tears from welling up. There they were, my two beautiful girls, running in the grass chasing a couple of butterflies. Their long blonde hair flew wild as they ran, and I couldn't help but laugh. They had definitely gotten their mother's hair.

The laugh caught their attention, and their eyes lit up like the sun when they saw me.

"Dada!"

I dropped to one knee and caught them as they ran into my embrace. I hugged them so tight and close and simply basked in their smell. I kissed their heads and kept hugging them.

"Daddy's home, my angels."

"For how long?"

"For good this time."

"Is that so?" my wife asked from behind me.

I let my girls go and stood to face her. She wore a grey skirt with a white top. Her hair was pulled up with a loose strand dangling in her face. Her eyes were wet with tears as well, and she was trying to be stern with me, but I could tell she missed me just as much as I missed her.

I took two steps forward and picked her up off the ground and spun her in the air. She let out a little squeal and the girls giggled. I let her feet touch the ground and pulled her close and kissed her. Her lips were warm and tasted slightly of peppermint.

"It's so," I said. "I promise. No more outlawin' for me. I'm done."

She didn't say any words, but her eyes told me everything. She hugged me tightly.

The girls resumed their pursuit of the elusive butterflies. I sat on the porch and wondered why I had ever left in the first place.

As I sat there, something caught my eye. Something nestled back in the hickory trees. I stood and walked towards it. It was white.

My legs began to shake as I walked. It couldn't be.

There, standing alone amongst the ancient hickory trees, was a lone aspen.

My girls ran towards me and their bones creaked and groaned.

Acknowledgments

I need to throw a huge shout-out to a few folks. First and foremost, my wife. She has supported me and my writing from the get-go, giving me the time I need to write. Second, my mom. I always give her my stories to read, and she gives me good, honest feedback. Her eye for detail is also next to none, and she can find the little things I miss. Next, I need to thank Caryn Larrinaga and Scott Forman. They are my beta readers and help me shape these stories into what they need to be. Following that, I need to thank the horror community and the fans. The support and love that come out of most of you are amazing and can fill this person's heart with the appropriate amount of darkness (the good kind of darkness, in this case). Thanks for supporting me and my writing. It means the world.

-C.R. Langille

About the Author

C.R. Langille spent many a Saturday afternoon watching monster movies with her mom. It wasn't long before she started crafting nightmares to share with her readers. She is a retired, disabled veteran with a deep love for weird and creepy tales. This prompted her to form Timber Ghost Press in January of 2021. She is an affiliate member of the Horror Writers Association, the DEI Chair for the League of Utah Writers, and she received her MFA: Writing Popular Fiction from Seton Hill University in 2014.□

Follow her here: https://link.heropost.io/crlangille

If you enjoyed, *Through the Branches*, please consider leaving a review on Amazon or Goodreads. Reviews help the author and the press.

If you go to www.timberghostpress.com you can sign up for our newsletter so you can stay up-to-date on all our upcoming titles, plus you'll get informed of new horror flash fiction and poetry featured on our site monthly.

Take care and thanks for reading, *Through the Branches* by C.R. Langille.

-Timber Ghost Press